The Wolf Chronicles

First Edition

Alan Weyant

The Wolf Chronicles

First Edition

Published by The Nazca Plains Corporation
Las Vegas, Nevada
2007

ISBN: 978-1-934625-10-1

Published by

The Nazca Plains Corporation ®
4640 Paradise Rd, Suite 141
Las Vegas NV 89109-8000

PUBLISHER'S NOTE
The Wolf Chronicles is a work of fiction created wholly by *Alan Weyant's* imagination. All characters are fictional and any resemblance to any persons living or deceased is purely by accident. No portion of this book reflects any real person or events.

Cover, Supraphoto
Art Director, Blake Stephens

Dedication

To Sloyd, my partner, my friend, and the love of my life. Thank you for your guidance, your strength, your encouragement, and the occasional swift kick in the butt! But mostly, thank you for your love.

The Wolf Chronicles

Alan Weyant

Contents

Chapter One
The Torture

Wolf's muscles rippled under his copper-bronze skin as I spread his arms and legs, fastening them with heavy leather restraints to the ends of the arms of the St. Andrew's cross in my dungeon. The sweat immediately began to bead up on his thick, sculpted pectorals and his washboard, six-pack abdominal muscles. It also started to trickle down his ribcage from Wolf's deep, stretched armpits. Months of heavy bodybuilding, proper diet, and supplements had transformed his solid, but formerly wiry, physique into a mass of ripped and sculpted muscle that would be the envy of many middleweight bodybuilders.

His cock began to swell as he thought of the tortures he would soon be forced to endure. It rose in a series of small, arcing jerks, until his cock stood fully erect, the eight-inch length throbbing slightly. The shaft bulged around the tight, shiny, stainless steel cock ring surrounding the base of his cock and balls. The veins that coursed the length of his dick pulsed with the rhythm of Wolf's heartbeat, and a drop of pre-cum glistened on the plum colored head.

I straightened up and faced my tightly bound slave boy, who stood helplessly awaiting whatever torture I decided to inflict upon his naked, spread-eagled body. For perhaps the thousandth time since I had first laid eyes on him in the San Francisco Eagle, I admired the lines of his handsome Amerindian / Latino face. He had high cheekbones and a long, angular jaw line, set off by a permanent faint five o'clock shadow and framed by the thick mane of raven black hair that flowed down over his shoulders and onto his chest, reaching past his thick, brown nipples. As I looked into his deep brown eyes, he silently looked back, his expression showing his desire to please me by giving his body to me to use in whatever way I desired.

I grabbed a handful of his glossy hair and yanked it hard, snapping his head back and forcing Wolf to look directly up into my eyes as I loomed over him. I loved the feel of the heat of his naked, helpless body as I pressed my bare chest against his. I also loved the look of fear mixed with lust that was in his eyes. I leaned in close to his face and growled; "Tell me what you want, slave."

He softly whispered back; "I want pain, Sir. Please, Master, torture me! Make me hurt, Sir! Make me scream and beg for mercy, Sir, please!"

On an impulse, I kissed him deeply. We stayed like that; our lips locked together, our tongues exploring each other's mouths, until I broke the kiss, Wolf moaning with lust as I withdrew from his face. Bending over, I started to suck and chew on each of his thick, erect nipples, causing him to moan and gasp with pain and pleasure. I knew that his tits were his most sensitive parts. He writhed and twisted on the cross, his body straining, moaning with ever more urgent lust, as I sucked and chewed harder and harder on the thick knots of sensitized flesh capping his solid pecs. I stood up and forced Wolf's face into my right armpit, dripping with my sweat.

"Lick it out, slave." I growled into his ear. I immediately felt the warmth of his tongue as he started licking and sucking the sweat out of my hot pit. I always kept the dungeon warm, as I loved watching a slave sweat as I tortured him. I also loved the look and feel of the sweat coating my own muscles. I let him lick my pit for just a few moments before I switched sides, forcing him to eat out my other armpit.

I rose up in front of his bound body, stroking my fingers over Wolf's tightly stretched torso, feeling every rock-hard muscle under his silky smooth skin. I twisted and pulled on his hard, dark brown nipples until he was writhing in ecstasy. A lucky combination of genetics had given Wolf a naturally dark golden brown skin color with almost no body hair, except for small tufts in each armpit, plus a small patch above his cock.

At last, I pulled away from him, before the desire to make love to him right there on the cross became too much to control.

Turning towards the shelves fastened to the wall that held part of my collection of toys, I picked up one of my favorite floggers, then turned back towards my helpless, bound slave boy. He whimpered softly at the sight of the cat-o-nine tails I was holding.

I reached out and brushed the hair hanging down over his chest back over his shoulders, snarling "I want to be able to get a clear shot at those pecs and tits with nothing in the way. You can beg all you want, but you'll get no mercy from me tonight, boy. I hope you're ready to suffer, slave, because I'm in the mood to hear you scream in total agony tonight!"

His only reply was a soft "Oh yes, Sir. Thank you, Sir."

I slowly draped the tails of the flogger across his tightly stretched chest, drawing them up across his face. His eyes closed in ecstasy as he inhaled the scent of the tanned leather, his chest expanding dramatically as he breathed in the erotic scent. I gathered up the ends of the tails and rubbed them against his mouth. At that, he went into an orgy of licking and chewing on the strands of leather that would soon be torturing him.

I let him enjoy this sensual pleasure for only a moment before pulling the flogger away, growling "You're having too much fun, boy. Now, it's time to pay."

He whimpered, "Yes, Sir, I'm sorry, Sir."

I swung the flogger, splaying the tails in a neat fan pattern across his chest. His eyes rolled back as he drew a sharp breath in through clenched teeth. Every muscle in his naked sculpted body tightened with the impact. Again and again, I slashed the tails of the cat across Wolf's torso, transforming the glistening skin to a deeper red, shading it into an angry reddish purple as welts began to rise across his rock hard pecs and his washboard six-pack abs. His chest rose and fell as he gasped for air between the burning impacts of the flogger, the sweat gleaming on his skin as though he had been oiled. His muscles bulged, straining against his bonds while he sobbed and whined continuously, a sure sign he was in the throes of a pain induced high.

After thoroughly torturing his torso with the flogger, I set it back on the shelf. Wolf gasped out a labored "Thank you, Sir."

Selecting a riding crop with an enlarged paddle end, I used it to torture Wolf's massive pectoral muscles and huge nipples, paddling them until his tits and pecs were a fiery red color. Wolf was keening softly, crying constantly from the pain.

I gnawed on his swollen, battered nipples again, until Wolf was screaming in agony. I closed in on him, our hot, sweat-covered bodies sliding against each other, kissing him deeply, fiercely; his screams muffled by my mouth until they died out.

The items I picked up next brought a loud wail of "Oh God, no!" from Wolf. That actually meant he wanted the pain he was about to experience. The alligator nipple clamps I held were possibly the most exquisitely painful torture devices I had yet used on his willing body. I squeezed one of the clamps open, allowing Wolf to see the double rows of sharpened metal teeth that would soon be biting at the flesh of his enlarged nipples. Months of vacuum pumping his nipples had given him engorged, dark brown tits that stood almost a full inch from his chest, as big around as his finger.

I placed the clamp on his right nipple, releasing the teeth to slowly close on the flesh of his already tender tit, biting into it with slowly building agony. Wolf closed his eyes, threw his head back and forth, growling, his breath hissing in through his gritted teeth. Finally, when the clamp was fully set on his tit, I repeated the procedure on his other nipple, setting off another round of growling and struggling.

I let Wolf pause for a moment as he absorbed the waves of pain that were coursing throughout his body. He once told me the alligator clamps felt to him like white-hot points of fire on his chest. To add to his torment, I hung small eight-ounce lead weights from the rings on the clamps that were savaging his tits. I leaned in to lightly flick my tongue across his tits, loving the hot salty taste of his sweat, mixed with the sharp tang of the metal tit clamps. Wolf moaned, straining his muscles at the teasing of his tits.

The next item I brought out of my toy collection caused Wolf to moan again even louder at the thought of more intense pain. I knelt down close to his body and cupped one hand around his hanging balls, pulling them down and stretching his scrotum. I wrapped the leather ball stretcher I held around his distended ball sack and buckled it into place. Wolf growled in his throat at the building level of pain in his nuts, as his body adjusted to this new source of torment.

Wolf whimpered when I handled another crop, this one with a small leather tip on the end. I flicked it across his tightly bound and rapidly swelling balls. I tortured his nuts for a good five minutes, slowly increasing the force of the blows with the crop, until Wolf was screaming in pain with each impact on his ball sack. I picked up a short length of heavy metal chain I had cut to the proper length for just this use, fastening it with a clip to the cross-strap that separated Wolf's nuts. Letting the chain hang from my torture slave's now incredibly tender balls caused him to grunt with each breath as the pain built in his lower gut.

"Do you like that, boy?" I sneered up at him, knowing that he was in equal parts agony and ecstasy. "Do you want more, boy?"

"Oh God, yes Sir!" he begged, looking down at me with a look of complete trust in his eyes. "Whatever you want to do to me, Sir. Please! Torture me, hurt me more, Sir, please!"

I grinned evilly up into his handsome face, now contorted by the extreme pain he was enduring, telling him, "O.K. You want more pain, boy, then more pain is what you will get." Wolf loved it when I told him that.

Wolf started to scream without restraint as I hung heavier weights from the chain, tugging his already tortured nuts even farther from his torso. I added one weight after another, each one drawing a howl from Wolf until I had an amazing total of twenty five pounds suspended from my slave's stretched, purple balls. His entire body was straining in bondage, every muscle rock hard, from his big biceps down to the solidly muscled towers of his legs.

To add to his suffering, I went to my toy box to get the case containing my collection of urethral sounds. Wolf shivered slightly as I smeared a large drop of lube on the tip of his cock and started to insert the thick rod of stainless steel into his cockhead. The metal shaft slowly slipped deeper and deeper into Wolf's twitching hard-on, until the sound was inserted the full eight-inch length of his dick.

I straightened up in front of my suffering slave, bending in to bury my face in his stretched, straining right armpit. I inhaled deeply, loving the hot man-smell of his pit. My two biggest fetishes were, first: men with long hair, which Wolf had in spades, and secondly: the look, taste, and smell of a hot, sweat-glazed muscular body.

I slurped my tongue into Wolf's armpit, shooting waves of ecstasy through his flesh, which only turned me on more. My mouth laved his armpit with spit, mixing it with the sweat on his skin. I graduated to nibbling, then biting the depth of his armpit. My tongue traced a path out of his armpit and up and over to his bulging bicep, following the veins standing out on the firm surface of his pumped muscle. I figured, since I owned his body, whatever I wanted to do with it was my choice.

Orally, I worshiped the muscle for a few minutes before switching to Wolf's other side, repeating the pit licking and muscle worship on Wolf's left side. When I had finished with Wolf's pits, I stood in front of his stretched, straining body, reaching out to his nipples. Wolf groaned in agony when I gently began to bounce the weights hanging from his nipple clamps with my fingers. He writhed as I tapped on the bottom of the weights, causing jolts of pain to rip through his already agonized nipples. After a few minutes of torturing my slave's nipples to the edge of his endurance, I retreated to let him process the pain.

I only let him rest for a moment before I started to gently stroke my hands over the hard washboard of his abs. My fingers tenderly rose and fell on the skin of Wolf's stomach. Gradually, I increased the force of my hands striking his skin. Ever so slowly, the tapping turned into light hits, then into firmer and firmer impacts, until I was slapping the reddening skin of my helpless slave's stomach with ever increasing force. I clenched my hands into fists, driving them into his abs, first one fist, then the other. His defined abs rippled between the blows. He choked out a strangled sounding "Thank you, Sir" after each punch, until he couldn't draw in enough air to speak. He was gasping for air as I started to pound my fists into his rock hard abs harder and harder. Within another minute, I was pummeling him as hard as I could, the sweat flying from his body with each blow, as he struggled to breathe between the impacts of my fists. Every movement of his body swung the weights hanging from his tits and balls, adding to his torture.

The beating continued for a few minutes, with Wolf gasping and grunting at each solid thud of my fists pounding deeply into his guts. Finally I stopped gut-punching my sagging, retching, struggling slave to watch him fight to breathe before he passed out, his stomach muscles heaving under his bright red skin.

I stepped to the chair I had in the dungeon and moved it in front of the cross to enjoy one of my favorite sights; my handsome, long haired, muscular pain pig enduring exquisitely painful torture. His head was thrown back, his eyes closed as he concentrated on fighting against the waves of agony ripping through his body. The breath rasped in Wolf's throat as he gasped for air through clenched teeth. His tautly stretched body strained against the restraints holding him spread-eagled, muscles tensing as he tried futilely to escape the bondage, the veins popping out on his bronzed physique from his neck all the way down to his massive thighs and sculpted calves. The sweat streaked down Wolf's body from his deep-corded armpits to his widely spread legs. I sat there admiring the view for a full fifteen minutes while my slave-boy could do nothing but endure the incredible torture he was being subjected to. I knew that he was mentally walking that razor edge between screaming in agony, and laughing in pure delight. The more pain he had to endure, the happier he was!

His cock hadn't softened a bit. If anything, the torture had actually caused it to get even harder. The head was swollen and purple, with long strings of pre-cum streaming out onto the dungeon floor from around the shiny metal sound protruding from his piss slit. The veins pulsed on the entire eight-inch length of his shaft.

At last he opened his eyes to look at me sitting in the chair in front of him, stripped down to my chaps and boots, my own body dripping with sweat from the exertions of torturing him in the heat of the dungeon. I stroked my own nine-inch, rock hard cock at the intensely erotic sight of his struggle to endure the torture without passing out from sheer pain.

"God, Sir, I love you", he gasped through his suffering. "I need more torture, Sir, please! Hurt me, Sir! Take me over the edge, please, Sir!"

Wolf's ability to endure pain was amazing. He was that rarest of all slaves, a true masochist who was totally sexually excited by the thought of extreme torture. He had the highest pain threshold I had ever seen. He could endure torture that would break almost any other man. I knew what he wanted me to do to him because we had discussed this scene for weeks, knowing it would mean Wolf would not be able to have an orgasm for several weeks afterward, until he healed fully.

"I know what you want me to do to you, boy," I told him. "Are you sure you want it?"

"Yes, Sir, please, Sir! I'm ready for it." He answered using a pleading tone I rarely heard from him.

"All right, boy," I told him. "Prepare yourself for the worst pain you have ever endured."

Standing, I slid the chair away from the cross and forced his face deeply into my armpits again. I let him clean out the sweat dripping down my flesh. Kneeling down, I fastened thick leather restraints around Wolf's massive thighs, totally immobilizing his legs. I added additional restraints to his arms as well, strapping them across his pumped biceps.

I positioned a small table just high enough that the top was about eight inches below Wolf's throbbing cock. On the table I placed a candle about six inches high with a flat base holding it upright. Wolf watched with an expression on his face that was part apprehension mixed with an equal part desire as I lit the candle. I waited for the flame to level out, slowly sliding the candle towards the throbbing, swollen head of Wolf's cock.

I held the flame under the end of the sound sticking out of his cock just long enough for a bit of heat to be transmitted up the metal shaft inside Wolf's dick, making him writhe and strain against his restraints. Finally, I slowly withdrew the shaft from his cock, Wolf moaning with lust at the feel of the warm metal sliding out of his cock.

I slowly ran the flame of the candle up and down the length of Wolf's swollen cock, not stopping, but moving the flame slowly enough so that he felt the heat without any actual damage being done. Wolf stared down at the sight of his cock apparently being slowly roasted, with eyes that were wide with fear and desire at the same time.

After a few more minutes of teasing his cock with the flame, I said to Wolf, "Are you ready for it, boy?"

"Oh yes, Sir, please, do it, Sir" he begged, his voice hoarse with a combination of lust and fear.

"All right, boy, here it comes," I told him. I pushed the candle in towards Wolf's body so that the flame engulfed the head of his cock and left it there! His entire body convulsed in raw agony as his cockhead started burning, the skin scorching and blistering.

Wolf threw his head back, screaming, "OH SHIT, MASTER, OH SHIT! OH MY GOD, SIR!" louder than I had ever heard him scream before, as every muscle in his entire body flexed and strained to their absolute limits! The leather of the restraints was actually creaking from the strain Wolf was subjecting them to.

Within seconds he shrieked, "OH GOD, I'M CUMMING, SIR!"

As he started to shoot thick wads of sperm from his burning cockhead, I reached out to open and remove the clamps from both of his nipples at the same time. Wolf's screams got even louder as I squeezed and twisted both of his battered nipples.

He shrieked, "OOOHH FUUUUUCCCK!! SON OF A BITCH!!" as I brutalized his tits.

Finally he shot one last stream of cum out of his blackened cockhead, which dripped down on the candle, putting out the flame to end Wolf's torture by fire.

I was so turned on by now I couldn't help pumping my own cock to an explosive orgasm, shooting my cum all over the front of my tortured slave. I dove in to push the table out of the way and licked the sweat from Wolf's deep armpits. He whimpered as I worked my tongue down his muscled torso, sucking up his sweat mixed with my own cum.

After several minutes, I looked up into Wolf's eyes to see raw agony mixed with pure love. Tears were streaming down his face as he whispered with the last of his strength, "I love you, Sir."

His eyes closed as he slumped down, supported only by the restraints around his arms and legs, having passed the point of his body's ability to endure the pain and shock of his burning. This was only the third time in the fourteen months that we had been together that I had tortured Wolf to the point of passing out from his pain. I unbuckled the ball stretcher from Wolf's swollen nut sack and rotated the cross from its vertical position to a horizontal one to make it easier to remove the restraints from Wolf's body. I hefted his limp, barely coherent form up to carry him to the cot I had in the corner of the dungeon.

When he awoke he was lying on the cot with bandages wrapped around his cock surrounding a catheter tube I had inserted before dressing his burns so he didn't have to hold his cock while pissing. Luckily, Wolf's cock wasn't really badly burned, as he had cum so soon after the flame touched his skin that he only had some smallish blisters. It had looked worse in the subdued lighting of the dungeon than it really was. I had spoken with several friends of mine who were doctors to determine the proper treatment for the type of damage Wolf's cock was going to suffer. I wasn't going to let my slave boy lover incur any permanent damage. I loved him too much to allow anything to happen to him. I leaned over him as soon as I saw he was awake and kissed him.

I asked him "How are you, boy?"

"Oh, my God, Sir, that was the most intense thing I have ever felt in my life, Sir! I loved it! Thank you, Master, oh thank you!"

"Do you think you can make it up the stairs to your room, boy? I think you'll be a lot more comfortable in your bed, boy."

Wolf nodded, then gingerly got to his feet. I helped support him as we slowly staggered upstairs. When he was comfortable in his bed, I bent over to kiss my exhausted, battered, burned, and totally happy slave again, telling him;

"Just think boy. Maybe the next time I'll use red-hot branding irons on your nipples," as I grinned evilly down at him.

"Oh yes, Sir, I can hardly wait!" he said, his eyes flashing with lust as he looked forward to his next torture by fire.

"Now, you need to sleep, boy." I told him gently, kissing him again.

Wolf murmured his assent and closed his eyes. I think he dropped off within a minute or two, as exhausted as he was after the intense tortures he had endured this night.

Wolf had no way of knowing I already had the branding irons for his tits fabricated; I was only waiting for the proper time to use them!

Chapter Two
The Meeting

Later that evening, as Wolf slept, exhausted after his torture by fire, I sat by his bedside watching him and marveling at his strength. No one else that I had ever tortured before would have been able to endure the severe pain and suffering that I had inflicted on Wolf's willing body. As I watched the gentle rise and fall of his thickly muscled chest as he breathed, I remembered back to our first meeting over a year earlier.

I had been sitting in the outdoor courtyard of the Eagle, enjoying a beer with a few friends of mine, including some other topmen with their slave boys. We were trying to cool off after an unusually hot early summer day. As we chatted and good-naturedly bitched about the heat, I saw a sight that made my temperature rise a few more degrees. Walking out of the main part of the bar into the courtyard was quite simply the most exotically handsome young man I had ever seen. As he walked through the crowd, I could see most of the guys in the courtyard turn and look at him admiringly. Something about the boy exuded a hot, erotic sexuality unlike almost anyone else I had ever seen. He was dark skinned, with a face that hinted of a mixed heritage, probably Latino and something else, as yet unknown, as evidenced by his eyes, which had an almost Asian cast to them, but with high, sculpted cheekbones and a long, tapered jaw. What had really caught my eye, however, was the fact that his handsome, chiseled face was surrounded with a thick mane of long black hair that hung down to the middle of his back, hair so black that it seemed to be highlighted with blue.

He was wearing a pair of denim cut-offs and combat boots with his keys hung on his right hip and a black bandanna in his right rear pocket. His slim, muscled upper body was barely covered with a sweat-soaked white tank top that clung to his skin like it had been painted on. Every muscle in his torso rippled as he walked straight towards where I was sitting with my friends. When the boy arrived in front of us he dropped down onto his knees, looked directly into my eyes and then bowed his head. Clasping his hands behind his back he said softly in a deep, but almost shyly hesitant voice; “Sir, may this boy have permission to speak to you?”

Thankfully, my friends went silent as I said to him “Go ahead, boy”

“Thank you, Sir. All this boy wanted to say was that he thinks that you are the handsomest man he has ever seen. This boy would consider it an honor to be able to serve you in any way possible, Sir.”

I sat for a moment, taken aback by this outright declaration of desire. Finally, I reached out and placing one hand under his chin, I lifted his head up so I could look directly into his deep, brown eyes. “All right, boy, for your first task, get me another beer. Go.”

“Yes, Sir.” He answered as he rose to his feet and started working his way through the crowd towards the bar.

My friends immediately started in ragging on me. “Hey, look at that, Eric’s got a new boy toy!” “Oh, Sir, you’re sooo handsome!” “What you gonna do with that, humm?”

“At least I know what to do with a boy like that. He obviously has good taste!” I shot back. “Which is more than I can say for any of you losers!” They all laughed and mockingly toasted me with their beers.

“Well, good luck with that hottie, anyway. Do you think he might last longer than any of the other so-called slave boys you have had to put up with?” said Danny Hendrickson, the lean, muscular redhead who was my best friend. “And by the way, who the hell is he?”

I had to admit, “I have absolutely no idea. I can’t ever remember seeing him in here before today. But, I guarantee I’m gonna do my damndest to get him into my dungeon to find out exactly how much he can take!”

At about that time, the boy arrived back where we were sitting, carrying a cold beer. Dropping to his knees, he held it out for me to take from him. “Your beer, Sir.” he said quietly.

“Thank you, boy.” I told him.

“Yes, Sir” he replied. “My pleasure, Sir.”

I took a deep draft of the beer and told the boy “Come with me, boy. We need to talk somewhere a little quieter, away from all the riff-raff!”

My friends razzed me good-naturedly as I rose to my feet and waited for the boy to stand. Waving a quick good-bye to my friends, I led the boy back towards an empty corner of the courtyard where there were some tables that weren’t occupied. I sat on one of the chairs and the boy immediately knelt at my feet, his head down.

“All right, boy, first things first. My name is Eric Kurtz, but you will call me ‘Sir’, unless I tell you otherwise. Is that understood, boy?”

"Yes, Sir", he replied instantly.

"Good. Now tell me about yourself. What's your name, boy?"

"My name is Carlos Greywolf, Sir."

"Interesting name. What is its derivation, boy?" I asked him.

"My mother was Mexican-American and my father was Apache Indian, Sir." That explained his exotic look that had so intrigued me from the start.

As we talked, he told me that his parents had been killed in an auto wreck almost a year earlier near his home in Arizona. He had been hitch hiking around the country ever since doing odd jobs, surviving on his wits and a modest inheritance left by his parents. He also told me he had arrived in town a week or so earlier and had seen me once or twice before in the bar but had stayed back in the shadows in the corners because he had been afraid to try to talk to me.

I frowned at that, telling him; "First lesson, boy. Never be afraid to talk to me or tell me something, even if you think that I won't like it. What will happen when I find out whatever it was you didn't tell me anyway? Will that make it easier on me and what do you think will happen to you when I find out that you were afraid to tell me? Besides, why on earth would you be afraid to talk to someone in a bar, especially a leather bar?"

"I was afraid you would reject me publicly and I didn't know if I could take that, Sir." he said softly, with an almost sobbing quaver in his voice, keeping his gaze fixed on my boots.

"Why would my rejecting you hurt you that badly, boy?" I asked him gently, truly intrigued by this mysterious boy.

He looked up at me and I was surprised to see tears streaming down his face. "Because, from the first time I ever laid eyes on you, Sir, I knew you were the master I was destined to serve for the rest of my life!" He looked back down at the ground, his shoulders slumping as though making that admission was one of the hardest things he had ever done.

I sat back, so truly stunned by this revelation that I couldn't say anything for at least a minute.

Finally, I asked him "How could you know that, boy?"

"I can't explain it fully, Sir. Maybe it has something to do with the fact that my Grandfather was a Shaman and claimed to have the ability to see into the future. Maybe I inherited a small bit of that power, if it truly exists, or maybe I'm just imagining it all, but all I know is that when I saw you, I just knew it, Sir", he softly said. He then looked back up into my eyes and gave me a crooked, slightly lopsided smile that seemed to light up his entire face.

I looked into his deep brown eyes, seeing only truth and honesty there, without any hint of duplicity. “Well, boy, after a revelation like that, I guess I will have to take you home with me. I don’t want to risk angering the gods.” I grinned at him to let him know I was teasing him a little but not making fun of him.

I got serious again when I asked him; “So you want to serve me any way you can, right, boy?”

“Oh yes, Sir, any way at all.” he breathed.

“Do you enjoy pain, boy? I see you’re flagging a black bandanna.” I looked directly into his eyes as I told him; “I am going to be totally honest with you, boy. I’m always honest with anyone that I’m with, and I expect them to always be honest with me at all times. What I am is a sadist, pure and simple. I enjoy causing other men extreme pain and watching them suffer. There will be a great deal of pain for you. I like to test my slaves and take them to the limits of what they can endure. All the other so-called slaves I have had haven’t been able to endure my testing. As a matter of fact, I don’t even like to refer to what I do as testing. I prefer to cut to the chase and call it exactly what it is. Torture.”

At the word “torture”, the boy’s body seemed to shiver. I noticed a twitch in the bulging fabric of the shorts over his crotch.

“Oh yes, Sir,” he moaned. “My biggest dream and deepest desire has been to find a master who will torture me to the limit and then take me over, Sir. I enjoy pain, Sir, and I enjoy being made to suffer extreme pain at someone else’s hands, Sir. I had friends tie me up and torture me ever since I was about fifteen years old, Sir, but I’ve never had a real master! Will you be that master, Sir, please?”

He looked deeply into my eyes and said; “Please, Sir, Will you torture me until I can’t take any more, and then keep going, please, Sir? I am willing to give my body to you to do whatever you want to me. I need to endure as much pain as I can, Sir, to prove my worth to you as your slave, Sir!”

I had to admit to myself that this was the first time I could ever remember that I had such a hot boy actually begging me to torture and hurt him. I instantly made a decision.

“If that’s what you want, boy, then that’s what you’re going to get.” I told him for what turned out to be the first of many times. I stood up directly in front of the kneeling boy and told him to clean my boots. He bent down and began licking my polished engineer boots. As he cleaned one boot and then the other, I slowly drew the handcuffs out of the case on the back of my belt and opened them up. At the distinctive clicking sound, the boy tensed but never missed a lick. I bent down and grabbed his right wrist, bent it behind his back and snapped the cuff on it. I heard a soft moan of desire come from the boy kneeling at my feet then I repeated the procedure with his left wrist, and was rewarded with another moan, leaving him bent over licking my boots with both arms fastened behind his back. I let him finish cleaning both of my boots before ordering him up.

"All right, boy" I told him, "Stand up."

He struggled to his feet in front of me, his head just coming up to the level of my chin. I reached out and grabbed the fabric of his tank top at the neck and, giving it a yank, tore the shirt from him, leaving him stripped to the waist, his smooth, dark, muscular torso glistening with sweat. Heads all over the courtyard turned at the sudden, sharp sound of the thin cotton tank top ripping apart. I took the sweat soaked, shredded shirt and stuffed it into his mouth, tying the ends of the tails around his head as a gag. The boy looked even hotter stripped to the waist than I had imagined that he would, the sweat shining on his sculpted pecs with their high riding brown nipples, his taut, washboard six-pack ab muscles glistening in the fading light of the late evening. Every rib rippled under his skin, which made me think that this boy couldn't have had more than five or six percent body fat. I could tell that he had done some serious bodybuilding in the past, even if he wasn't currently working out. I was really looking forward to a night of extreme torture for this young stud.

"Follow me, boy," I told him. I gave a nod to my friends as we walked past them, but I could feel their eyes following us as we headed towards the front door of the bar. The crowd in the front section of the bar parted as we walked through, as most of the leathermen there knew what we were going out to do. I smiled to myself when I heard a couple of guys whispering things like; *"Holy Shit. That figures! Leave it to Eric to end up leading that hot stud boy out, the lucky bastard! How the hell does he do it?"* and *"Jesus, would you look at the body on that stud! That hot little son-of-a-bitch isn't built, he's fucking carved!"*

I led the handcuffed and gagged boy outside into the parking lot, and pushed him into the rear compartment of my '55 Nomad wagon. I covered him with a blanket, partly to block his vision, adding to his feelings of helplessness, partly to hide a half naked, gagged and handcuffed man from any other motorists.

I took my time driving home, using a less direct route than usual, to thoroughly confuse the boy tied up in the back to keep him from figuring out where I was taking him, and to add to his feelings of anticipation of what I was going to do to him.

When we arrived at my home in the hills above Sausalito, I led the still handcuffed and gagged boy into my dungeon space, built into the underground garage space under the main part of my home. The boy's eyes widened as he took in the sight of my extensively equipped blackroom. Within a few minutes I had the boy spread-eagled, naked except for his boots and a plain black leather training collar locked around his throat, in chains standing between two pillars in the center of the dungeon. When I untied the shirttails from around his head and pulled the rest of the shirt from his mouth his only comment was a soft "Thank you, Sir."

I reached out and grabbed a fistful of his thick black hair with one hand and slapped both of his cheeks with the other just hard enough that the boy gasped in shock. I leaned in close to his face. "Did I give you permission to speak, boy?" I snarled at him.

"N-No, Sir, I-I-I'm sorry, Sir"; he stammered.

"Second lesson, boy. Just remember, that as of right now you are now my property and all you can do without my express permission is breathe and blink your eyes, and you might even need my permission to do that sometimes!" I let go of his hair and stepped back from him. "Just consider your situation, boy. You're chained up in a strange dungeon, where almost no one except for my friends at the bar knows where you are and you are about to endure extreme torture at the hands of someone you have just met. How does that make you feel? Now you can speak, boy."

He looked both apprehensive and excited as he said, "It makes me feel frightened and really turned on at the same time, Sir."

I saw from looking down at his swollen cock that he was truly turned on by the thought of the imminent torture. I ran my hands down across the planes of his torso, marveling at the feel of the warm, silk-smooth skin covering his chest and ab muscles and his rippling ribs. I spent a few moments twisting and pulling on his brown nipples, causing expressions of pain and pleasure to alternate on his handsome face as moans of pleasure escaped from his lips.

"So, you feel frightened, boy? That's good. It shows that you are smart enough to recognize your situation, boy." I stepped away from him and turned towards the door that led upstairs. "I'm going to let you think about what is going to happen to you for a while, boy." I opened the door and started up the stairs. "Oh, just so you will find it easier to concentrate on your situation, I'm going to eliminate any distractions." I told him as I flipped off the lights, leaving him chained up in total darkness.

Closing the door, I went upstairs to change into clothes more appropriate for torturing my new slave. I left him in total darkness for about three quarters of an hour while I changed and fixed myself a cup of tea to counter the effects of the two beers I had at the bar, which was my self-imposed limit. I wanted to be totally in control of myself during the upcoming session with my new boy. I was starting to realize that this boy could be something special, not like a lot of the one-night stands I had experienced recently.

When I returned to the dungeon, my new boy drew in a sharp breath at his first sight of me after I flipped on the lights. When I had gone upstairs, I was wearing denims, a leather vest and engineer style boots, but no shirt, since it was a hot night. When I returned, I was attired in leather chaps, a chest harness, knee high polished biker style boots, and a jock pouch. He looked like he wanted to say something, but apparently he remembered my admonition about talking out of turn, so he remained silent. I walked over to him and stood in front of his stretched body.

I stood there for a few minutes, my arms crossed on my chest, just staring into the boy's eyes until he looked down, properly cowed and submissive.

I grabbed a handful of his thick, black hair, snapped his head back, leaned in closely and snarled into his ear; "First things first, boy. You understand that I now own you, body and soul. I can make your life a living hell, or I can provide you with pleasure unlike anything you have ever experienced. It's up to you. Behave like a proper slave and life will be good. Screw up and you will wish you had never walked into the bar today."

Turning towards my toy rack, I picked up a cat-o-nine tails and, turning back towards him, told the boy; "Time for your next lesson in slavery, boy. We're going to find out if you really do want to be tortured, or if you're just another bullshit wannabe slave!"

I pushed his hair forward and began to work the cat across Carlos' back and shoulders, watching the muscles flex and seem to flow under his skin. I started slowly, as I always did with a new boy, until I could tell how he would respond to the flogging. As I slowly increased the force of the whipping, Carlos seemed to grow stronger right along with it. That was another clue that I had encountered a truly remarkable individual, one that was destined to change my life for the better!

That night, my new boy endured over three hours of intense tortures ranging from flogging with the cat-o-nine tails to a whipping with a single tail whip on both his back and his chest. He was then moved to the bondage table, where the torture continued. He endured intense nipple tortures, including his first extended nipple pumping session, and nipple electrification with the TENS unit and my U.V. wand, and cock tortures ranging from a cock flogging with a small cat made just for that purpose, to having increasingly thicker, long metal sounds inserted up the head of his thick, dripping cock while his cockshaft was covered with rubber coated clothespins. His balls were clamped in a portable vise, slowly enduring more and more pressure on his nuts, until they must have felt like they were being crushed totally flat.

By the time we were done for the night, Carlos was on his knees in front of me, moaning with pain, with his hands restrained behind his back by a pair of wrist restraints attached to a wide leather strap running down from a bondage collar fastened around his throat, with his ankles shackled together, while the sweat poured down his naked, welted body. His hair was matted with sweat and stuck to his back and shoulders. Surprisingly, though, his cock was fully hard, as it had been throughout the entire torture session.

I left him bound on his knees in the middle of the floor while I walked over to the master's chair in one corner of the dungeon. Sitting down, I ordered my new slave to lie belly down on the rough concrete, and crawl over to me like the worm that he was.

Slowly, he painfully dragged himself over to me, inching along on the harsh, unyielding floor. Finally, he worked his way to my feet, panting and gasping with the effort, and the pain of the rough concrete abrading the already tender skin of his naked body.

Since he had done what I asked willingly, without any hesitation, I rewarded him by allowing him to spend about ten minutes licking my boots before I stood up in front of him, and hauled him back onto his knees by grabbing a handful of his thick, raven hair.

I told the boy to open his mouth so I could drive my throbbing cock into that incredibly hot orifice. His mouth was so good, his sucking so intense, that I shot a huge load deeply into his throat within minutes. Carlos swallowed what turned out to be the first of many loads of my cum. I released him from his bondage and we went upstairs where I told him to wash me in the shower, then to clean himself up.

After we had showered, while lying in my bed together, I wrapped my arms around the still trembling boy after he had cried himself out, and softly asked him; "Well, boy, was it what you wanted?"

He turned to face me and softly moaned; "Oh God, yes Sir. It was all that and more, Sir."

"Well then boy, I guess we had better make it permanent, don't you think?"

Carlos looked at me for a moment, then tears started trickling down his face. He softly said; "Oh God yes! Thank you, Master, thank you!" He lowered his head down and began to weep harder, his tears dripping onto my chest.

"O.K. boy. First change in your new life. As of now your name is "Wolf".

It's shorter than Carlos, and it sounds better for a slave. Understood, boy?"

He smiled at me and replied "Yes Sir. My name is Wolf, Sir."

Since he had done such a good job of enduring the heavy tortures I had subjected him to that night, I decided to give him a bit of a reward, allowing him to jack his tender cock off on my chest and abs, then let him lick his cum off of my body.

Normally, I would never think of asking a boy to live with me after just one session together, but there was something indefinably special about Wolf that I had sensed the very first instant I had seen him.

The next day, Wolf and I went to his motel room, collecting his belongings to move into my house. He was clad only in his cut off denim shorts and boots, since I had shredded his shirt the night before in the bar, his bare chest and back still criss-crossed with whip marks and welts from the floggings he had endured. I told him to walk into the lobby of the motel dressed like that to see if he was truly ready to obey my orders in public. He did as I ordered without the slightest bit of hesitation. When we arrived back at my house, I instructed him to put his belongings in one of the spare bedrooms. When he was done, I called him into my room and ordered him to kneel in front of me. I buckled a wide, studded leather slave collar around his throat.

As I snapped the padlock on the locking post of the collar, I looked down into his deep brown eyes, glistening with tears of joy, as I told him; "Welcome to your new life as my slave, boy. Your training begins right now. You will do whatever I tell you to do, whenever I tell you to do it. Any hesitation or argument will not be allowed. I will never tell you to do anything, or will I do anything to you that will injure you, but you will suffer pain. You will only speak when spoken to, and then you may only answer directly. You are not allowed the use of any of the furniture in the house. You must earn that right. Any mistakes or transgressions will be severely punished. You are a slave, boy. That makes you about three steps less than human, in my eyes, until you can prove differently to me. Do you understand these rules, and do you agree to them, boy? Don't think that these are all the rules you will have to obey, slave. These are just the basics, boy. There will be a more detailed list later."

He silently nodded his head and softly said; "Yes, Sir. I agree to obey all your rules, Sir. I understand that I am now your property and that you are now my Master. You may do whatever you will with me, Sir. I no longer exist as a person, only as a slave until you have decided that I have earned the right to be a person again. My body is yours, Sir, do with it what you wish, Sir."

Wolf silently bent down and began licking my boots as his new life as my slave began.

My reverie ended when I started in my seat next to Wolf's bed, realizing that I had almost fallen asleep. I stood up and leaned over the bed, gently kissing him on the cheek. He murmured softly in his sleep as I quietly walked to the door of his bedroom. As I was leaving the room, I stopped and smiled at my slave as I whispered; "Sleep well, Wolf. You've earned a rest."

I closed the door and went to bed.

Chapter Three
Racked

In the weeks following Wolf's torture by fire, both he and I grew increasingly restless waiting for his burns to heal to the point we could again have a hard session in the dungeon without endangering his still healing cock. Luckily he wasn't as badly burned as I thought he would be at first since his skin was exposed to the flame for only a few seconds before his orgasm had extinguished the fire. But still, we had to wait for almost a week and a half before we could even make do with Wolf sucking my cock to orgasm and swallowing my hot load of cum two or three times a day, plus our regular sessions of nipple pumping to keep Wolf's tits swollen and tender. From the first day that we met, Wolf always told me that his greatest pleasure came from intense nipple torture. He loved any form of pain, but the sensations from extreme tit work were the most intense.

As satisfying as the pumping sessions were, and as good of a cocksucker that Wolf was, there was something missing that we both felt. Even our sessions of bodybuilding at the local gym had to be lighter than usual, at least for Wolf, as he had to be careful of his still tender cockhead. I could have worked over Wolf's back and ass with my floggers, but I preferred to play it absolutely safe and wait. I didn't want to run even the slightest risk of Wolf suffering any permanent damage. Plus, it was still painful for Wolf to get an erection, as it stretched the still healing skin of his dick, which was the reason we had no sexual contact at all the first ten or eleven days after his burning.

We continued our other activities however, such as working on the latest addition to my antique car collection, a 1931 Cadillac roadster, but sex was out for a while.

Finally after about three weeks and several visits to my doctor to check on his healing process, I decided that he was healed enough for play, as long as there wasn't any direct cock torture. As a result, that evening I called Wolf into my bedroom and ordered him to strip. He immediately obeyed, as he always did when I ordered him to do anything. I then gave him a pair of tight leather side snap briefs to put on.

I told him, "These are so your cock won't get damaged any more than it has, boy. At least not until I decide that it needs more damage!"

"Yes, Sir, thank you, Sir." He answered.

I could see that he was already anticipating a session in the dungeon, his cock beginning to lengthen and thicken even as he pulled on the tight briefs.

After I cuffed his hands behind his back, I told him to kneel and keep his head down while I changed into my leathers for the session. I put on my skin-tight chaps with a leather jock pouch, my lace-up logger boots, my vest, studded bands around each bicep, and my wrist gauntlets. I knew that this combination of skin and tight black leather always turned Wolf on, almost as much as the actual torture he had to endure. When I allowed him to look up again, he gave his usual anticipatory gasp with a soft moan of pleasure at the sight of me. I stood in front of him, 6' 2" tall, and 200 pounds as compared to his 5'7" and 170 pounds, 32 years old to his 24, with my spiked, buzz cut dark blonde hair contrasting with Wolf's thick black mane that flowed from his head down his body to the middle of his broad, tapered back and hung below his thick, pumped nipples in front. I also had the silver rings hanging from each of my dark brown nipples, while Wolf hadn't had his tits pierced, at least not yet. The only way that we resembled each other was in the dark golden brown color of our skin, natural for Wolf, the result of lots of tanning sessions for me, also, the way both of our bodies tapered from broad, muscled shoulders down to narrow waists, a result of long sessions of heavy bodybuilding in the gym. We both had the bodybuilding trophies to show for our efforts, mine from some local contests in San Francisco, Wolf's from a high school contest from his home town in Arizona.

"Stand up, boy" I told him, "Turn around".

Wolf immediately did as he was told, giving his usual shiver of anticipation as he did. He was always so turned on by the thought of a session of torture that he was unable to suppress the shiver, so I let him indulge in it.

To tell the truth, the thought that he was so ready to go even gave me a bit of a rush, too. I slipped his collar around his throat and locked it into position. I pulled his face to my chest and ordered Wolf to suck on my nipples. I allowed him his pleasure for just a moment before pulling him back from my chest. Hooking his leash to the collar, I told him; "Come on, boy, it's time for you to pay for lying around for the last few weeks."

"Yes, Sir" he softly answered.

I led him down the stairs into the dungeon, into the middle room and across to the far wall. He moaned softly when he saw where I was taking him.

"That's right. It's the rack for you this time, slave." I snarled into his ear.

He stood silently as I removed the handcuffs from his wrists and replaced them with thick, padded leather restraints. I told him to climb onto the rack and lie down. After he had clambered up onto the rack, I fastened the ankle restraints on the rack around Wolf's ankles, telling him to stretch his arms out over his head. When he did, I attached the wrist restraints to the chains wrapped around the drum attached to the winch on the end of the rack. I turned the crank just enough to pull Wolf's arms taut without stretching him yet. His chest lifted and spread, causing every muscle in his torso to stand out in sharp relief under his deep bronze skin. I could see a faint sheen of sweat already starting to appear on his skin, which just added to the definition of his magnificent musculature.

I slowly stroked my fingertips down over the satiny smooth skin of Wolf's body, admiring the feel of his warm skin and the look of the skin being stretched tightly over his thick, bulging ribcage. Every rib rippled under his golden brown skin as I gave his nipples a twist, causing him to moan with pleasure. I put my fingers up to his mouth and told him "Lick, boy."

He immediately began licking his own sweat from my fingers until I told him, "Enough, boy. Now it's time for you to suffer!"

I stepped back from the rack to strip off my vest, leaving me dressed only in chaps, boots, bicep and wrist bands, plus a leather jock pouch. I took hold of the crank on the winch of the rack and began to slowly turn it, drawing the chains tighter. Wolf's muscles began to tighten and flex against the slowly increasing strain being placed on his body. The ratchet mechanism on the winch clicked once, signifying the first one half inch of stretch of Wolf's body. I knew he could endure four inches of total stretch, but unknown to him, today we were not going to stop until I had drawn him out a full six inches. He groaned as the ratchet clicked again, for another half inch of pull. The sweat started to run down my chest from the effort of turning the winch crank against the strength of Wolf's magnificent physique. His body was also bathed in sweat from the slowly building pain that was gathering in his back and shoulders from being stretched. I turned the crank enough for another click, which caused Wolf to groan loudly. His torso was slowly being drawn tighter and tighter, drawing his stomach flatter, and causing his ribcage to bulge even more above his abs.

"All right, boy, now for something else to think about." I told him, picking up a pair of nylon crocodile clamps from the workbench next to the rack. Wolf growled deep in his throat as I attached the clamps to his thick nipples, setting the pressure on the clamps tight enough that Wolf's tits were squeezed tightly between the serrated teeth of the clamps. I attached the clamps to cords that ran up to small pulleys hanging from the ceiling beams. Looping the cords through the pulleys, I drew them taut, stretching Wolf's nipples away from his thick pecs. I tied the ends of the lines to eyehooks screwed into the next beam in the ceiling. Wolf's breathing became labored as the lines pulled his nipples tight.

"Now for some fun, boy!" I told my slave, watching his expression change from pain to anticipation as I hung a five-pound weight on each of the lines stretching his tits. He groaned again as the weights drew his nipples further away from his chest. He had just enough time to adjust to the new pain when I turned the crank on the rack another click, causing Wolf to finally scream with pain. "What's all that about, boy?" I taunted him, "You're only at two inches. We have another four to go, boy!"

He gasped "Oh, God, Sir, six inches? I don't think I can take all that, Sir!"

I knew that Wolf was saying that for my benefit, as we both knew that his appetite for extreme pain was almost insatiable. He screamed again as I forced the winch another click.

"Two and a half inches, boy, only partway there!"

"Oh yes, Sir, please stretch me more, Sir!" he moaned.

"That's more like it, boy. I don't want to hear any more of that 'can't take it' talk from you, boy. You'll take whatever I do to you, and like it, slave!" I snarled down at him.

"Yes, Sir, I'll take anything for you, Sir!" He was turning me on so much that I finally couldn't stand it any more. I hung another five pound weight from each of the tit ropes and then, while Wolf was gasping and moaning to adjust to this new pain, I leaned in and started running my tongue into his left armpit, licking and sucking on his sweat soaked skin. I loved the taste of Wolf's body, especially during the middle of a hot torture session. I always thought that his sweat had a faintly spicy taste to it. He flexed his muscles as I nibbled and chewed on the skin of his hot, deep armpit. I pulled on the wiry black hairs of his pit with my teeth, causing Wolf to struggle even harder. Finally I stood up over my stretched slave and leaned over him, kissing him deeply on the mouth. I felt his tongue flicking inside my mouth, licking out any traces of his own sweat. Crossing to the other side of the rack, I repeated the licking and pulling on his other pit, and kissed him again. I looked down at my suffering slave, then just to watch his reaction, I put my hands under the weights hanging from the ropes and lifted them up, relieving some of the pressure on his nipples. Wolf moaned softly as the pulling lessened on his tits, then he howled with pain and shock when I dropped the weights, jerking on his already tender, stretched nipples.

"Oh, God, Sir, please pull me harder, Sir, I want you to pull my arms out of joint if you want to, Sir. Please, Sir, I need more pain!" Wolf was begging me to increase the level of torture he was enduring. I was so turned on by his pleas that I turned the handle on the winch a full two clicks, drawing another deep-throated scream from him, "OH SHIT, YES SIR, MORE PLEASE, SIR!"

Wolf was almost sobbing by now as he begged me to hurt him more. I added another five pounds of weight to each of the ropes pulling on his nipples and forced the winch handle another click. Wolf screamed in agony, as this was as far as I had ever pulled him apart on the rack. "Do you want me to stop, boy?" I asked him.

"Oh please, no Sir" he whimpered. "Pull me more, Sir, please! Torture me, Sir, please hurt me as much as you can, Master! I will take whatever pain you want to give me, Sir!"

"All right, boy. You want more pain, more pain is what you will get!" I took the winch handle and began to turn it slowly, fighting against the incredible tension on my slave boy's body. Wolf began to shriek as I succeeded in getting another click out of the winch. He was now stretched tighter then he had ever been. Every muscle in his chest, stomach, and thick legs strained under his sweat-soaked skin and the tendons in his armpits looked like they were going to pop out any second. The hollow at the base of his ribs was now so deep that I could actually wrap my fingers around the bottom of his ribcage. His stomach was stretched so tightly that his abdominal muscles were now no more than six inches from his spine. God, he was unbelievably sexy! His handsome face was contorted in raw agony, his eyes squeezed tightly shut, as the breath rasped in and out of his throat.

I told him "I have to do this, boy; I just can't stand it any longer!" I reached out and removed the weights from his nipple ropes then unclipped the biting clamps that were torturing his tits. He screamed at the sudden rush of pain in his chest, screaming even louder as I kneaded the tender flesh of his tits between my fingers. I leaned over him, taking his right nipple in my mouth. Wolf moaned with pleasure as I sucked and nibbled on his swollen tit. His moans of pleasure began to turn to cries of pain as I began to bite harder on the mound of now exquisitely tender flesh. I tortured Wolf's nipple with my teeth for a good five minutes, enjoying the sounds of agony being torn from his throat, and the taste of his hot, sweaty chest before I switched sides, chewing on his other tit.

Finally I stood up and reached down to unsnap the briefs Wolf was wearing, allowing his swollen cock to spring free in an arc up over his rippled stomach. The head of his dick was still a bit redder than usual from his burning, but that was the only visible reminder of our last torture scene. I climbed up onto the rack to sit straddling Wolf's chest. I removed my jock pouch, freeing my nine-inch cock, which now pointed directly at Wolf's mouth.

"Open up, boy" I told him. He immediately opened his mouth as wide as he could. I lifted myself up so I could slide my cock into that hot, sucking mouth as far as possible. Wolf immediately began tonguing and nibbling on my thick shaft, as I began fucking his mouth. The sweat was dripping off of my chest down onto Wolf's face as I drove my cock into his mouth faster and faster. I fucked Wolf's mouth for a good ten minutes, driving my cock deeply into that hot hole, while my helpless slave worked my cockshaft with his tongue as fast as he could.

Gasping for breath, I told Wolf: "Take a deep breath, boy. We're going to see how long you can go without air!"

Wolf loved it when I controlled his breathing, but I had never done it to him in the middle of such agonizing torture. I felt his chest expand to its limit as I sat upright, and grabbing a handful of his hair, I pulled his head forward. I drove my cock deep into his throat, clamping my legs tightly on either side of his head, immobilizing it and cutting off any chance of his breathing. He immediately began to work my cockshaft as best as he could with his tongue. I felt him begin to struggle beneath me as his need for air began to grow more urgent with each passing second. I kept my cock buried in his throat as his body began to flex and strain in a rapidly mounting agony of imminent suffocation. He strained harder the longer I denied him the air he so desperately needed. I watched his increasingly desperate fight to breathe in the mirrors mounted on the wall of the dungeon next to the rack. I reached behind my butt to grab Wolf's nipples and began to torture them with my fingers as hard as I could, twisting and squeezing the tender knobs of flesh.

After at least 90 seconds without air while enduring the nipple torture, Wolf's struggling had reached the point of absolute frenzy. His muscles bulged and flexed, the veins popping out on his biceps and forearms, even across his pecs and thighs. His chest heaved under my ass as he desperately sought the air that I forced him to do without for at least another minute. His abs flexed, seeming to flow as he struggled to the limits of his strength against the chains holding him tightly stretched, against the cock blocking his frantic efforts to breathe. He moaned around the cock stuffed deeply into his throat.

Even while enduring almost unbearable multiple tortures at the same time, his cock hadn't softened a bit. The effort of enduring the incredible strain on his joints from the rack, the constant twisting and pulling on his already sensitive nipples, and the thick cock in his throat forcing him to do without air had caused Wolf's cock to swell and harden, the swollen head turning an almost purple color.

Finally I couldn't hold back any more against the urge to cum. With a loud yell, I shot a hot load of my sperm deeply into his willing mouth. Again and again I shot until I was totally drained. When I had pumped the last of my load into Wolf's throat I finally pulled out, allowing him to take a deep, shuddering gasp of air for the first time in almost three minutes.

"Oh my God, Sir, That was incredible" he gasped, when he could finally speak. "I was on the verge of either passing out or cumming myself, Sir."

"Well, let's see if we can get you off, boy!" I stood up next to the rack and with one hand grabbed Wolf's balls, squeezing them tightly while I twisted his nipples with the other. He shrieked as I rolled his balls against each other and pulled his tits like I was trying to rip them off his chest.

"OH SHIT, SIR!" he screamed, as his cock erupted with thick, ropy streams of jizz spraying across his straining torso, splashing onto his own face. Not being allowed to cum for weeks, he had built up a huge load. He licked as much of his own cum off his own lips as he could reach with his tongue. I ran my hand across the sweat-soaked planes of his muscled torso, smearing his cum and sweat together, holding my hand in front of his face for him to lick clean. He licked and sucked every drop of his cum I offered him off my hand, until I had cleaned all the semen from his body.

"Thank you, Sir", he panted, his chest still heaving and falling from the exertions of his explosive orgasm.

"Oh, you think we're done, do you, boy?" I leered down at him. He just looked up at me expectantly, awaiting whatever I wanted to do to him. Unexpectedly I grabbed the winch handle and gave it another pull, getting another two clicks out of the ratchet. Wolf shrieked at the top of his lungs at the unexpected burst of agony in his back and shoulder joints.

"OH SHIT!! OH-OH FUCK-OH MY GOD!! SIR, PLEASE STOP! RED-LIGHT!" he screamed, using our safe word, something he very rarely did. At that, I immediately released the ratchet lock on the winch and slowly eased the pressure on his body, so as not to hurt him by too sudden a release of the strain.

"Oh shit, thank you, Sir!" he moaned. "I'm sorry, I'm sorry, Sir, I just couldn't take any more, Sir, I'm sorry."

"Don't be sorry, boy," I told him. "I'm glad you had enough guts to use the word and not injure yourself for my sake, boy"

He was sobbing with pain and relief as I helped him sit up on the rack.

"Just take your time, boy. Take your time." He sat there for a few minutes as his body recovered from the unbelievable stress it had been under.

Finally he said, "May your slave thank you for his torture, Sir?"

"Go ahead", I told him. He rose to his feet and then knelt in front of me and began to lick my boots. I looked down at his broad, muscled back and shoulders, quivering from the strain he had endured, gleaming with the sweat of torture, his thick mane of raven black hair flowing over his back. I immediately fell even deeper in love with this incredible man!

After a few minutes of his bootlicking, I told him to stand up. When he did, I wrapped my arms around his tortured body and held him close to support him both physically and emotionally as I always did after a hard torture session. I felt him start to shake and shudder in a delayed reaction to the extreme agony he had endured. I held him closer as the sobbing started, the tears running down his cheeks, dripping onto my bare chest.

"It's O.K., boy. I'm here for you." I told him. "Go ahead and let it out!" I held him until the shaking of his body calmed, his breathing slowed to normal.

"Come on, boy, let's go upstairs and take a hot shower, then I'll put you to bed. If you are really good, I'll spend a few hours fucking you! It'll take me a while to cum again but I think you'll like the wait." I grinned down at him.

"Yes, Sir, thank you, Sir." He smiled at me with that slightly lopsided smile that I loved.

We went up the stairs into the house, and after a quick rinse off in the shower, we spent the next hour with my cock buried deeply in Wolf's tight, hot ass. At least twice I pumped him until I was on the brink of an orgasm and then cooled off a bit, prolonging the session, forcing Wolf to suffer, waiting for me to cum. He was begging for my sperm by the time I decided to give him my load.

When I finally started to cum inside of Wolf's ass, he hollered; "Oh fuck, Sir! Give it to me, please, Master!" He hollered even louder when I started to pull on his tender nipples while I coated the inside of his ass with my hot load.

Finally I pulled out of him; my orgasm spent, and flopped back down on the bed. Wolf immediately took my cock into his mouth, running his tongue over the incredibly sensitive head to clean it off. I moaned in ecstasy at the feel of his tongue, but finally had to tell him; "Enough, boy!"

Wolf just looked up at me with a devilish twinkle in his eyes. He knew what he was doing!

I pulled him down on top of me, loving the feel of my hands stroking up and down his sweat-coated, rock hard back and shoulder muscles, the heat of his chest pressed against mine, his hair flowing down over both of us, and told him; "Just remember, boy, paybacks can be hell! You just earned yourself two hours of the worst torture imaginable for a masochist!"

Wolf looked down at me and asked; "What's that, Sir?"

I told him; "I'll chain you up in the cell in the dungeon, describe all the tortures you are going to have to endure, and then leave you alone. No pain, no suffering at all!"

Wolf rolled his eyes in mock horror, "Oh God, Sir, anything but that, Sir!"

We both broke up in a laughing fit. After minutes of laughter, I told Wolf; "Let's hit the shower again and get some sleep, boy."

As we snuggled up together, the last thing I remember hearing before dropping off was Wolf's soft, "Good night, Sir, thank you for torturing me. I love you."

I wondered briefly if Wolf would feel that way in another week or so!

Chapter Four
Afternoon

The next morning, or to be more accurate, the next afternoon, I awoke from a deep, satisfying sleep to a wonderful, warm sensation on my chest. Wolf was curled up next to me on my left side as I lay flat on my back on the bed, his left arm lying across my chest, playing with the ring in my right nipple and stroking my thick pecs as he sucked on my left nipple. I lay there for a while enjoying the sensations of the warmth of his hard body and the feel of his muscles pressed against me, his hot mouth and tongue as they worked on my chest, his strong, but gentle fingers, also loving the feel of his long, silken hair spread across my body. Finally I opened my eyes, stroked my fingers down his hair and over his broad back and thick shoulders, and said, "Hi, boy, how are you feeling today?

He sighed, "Oh God, Sir! Last night was incredible, Sir! Thank you for torturing me, Sir, I missed it so much. I hurt so good today, Sir!"

He snuggled down closer to my side, running his tongue through my armpit and across my thick, 21" bicep. One of the things I loved about Wolf was the fact that he had learned how to sometimes know what I wanted without my having to say a word to him. Wolf loved to worship my muscles whenever I allowed him to, and I was feeling very generous today. Usually the morning after a hot dungeon session, I was mellow and relaxed, which was the exact opposite of Wolf. He still buzzed with endorphins; full of excess energy. The emotional release of torturing a hot man was incredibly fulfilling to me. I was in a wonderful mood this morning after torturing my handsome slave boy/lover for the first time in quite a while. That was why I wasn't going to say anything to Wolf about starting to make love to me or touching my body without express permission, since I figured that even though it was a breach of discipline for a slave, it was fully O.K. for my lover.

I slowly rolled over onto my stomach, allowing Wolf to climb up on top of me and sit across my butt. I groaned at the feel of his strong hands starting to work on the thick, taut muscles of my shoulders and back, digging gently but deeply into the muscles. I could feel the tension and aches slowly disappearing as Wolf gave me a wonderfully relaxing, sensual massage. He slowly worked his way down to my lower back. Wolf slid down onto my legs and began to massage my butt, first one side, and then the other. I let him work on my back for about ten minutes or so before I told Wolf that it was enough for right now, but he had one more surprise for me. I groaned at the feel of his hot tongue tracing my spine all the way from my neck down to the crack of my ass as he licked a thin bead of sweat from my skin, accompanied by the gentle, almost spidery feel of his hair on my back.

Finally he sat up and slid off to one side on the bed, allowing me to slowly turn back over. I had other plans for my boy for that day.

Wolf knew that if I wanted him to stop all I had to do was tell him to, but I slowly stretched and flexed my muscles then lay back with my hands under my head, luxuriating in the feel of release, silently signaling to Wolf that it was all right to continue. Wolf climbed up to straddle me again, sitting across my abs this time, a soft moan escaping his lips.

Wolf leaned forward to gently stroke his fingers over my spread torso, from my biceps and armpits all the way down to my abs. He reached behind his butt and ran his fingers lightly down my thighs as far as he could stretch. When he was done, he sat back upright to play with my nipples and my rings again. I moaned and closed my eyes for just a few moments, enjoying the sensual delight of gentle nipple play before I whispered, “Enough, boy. Now it’s your turn.”

I looked up at him sitting naked across my abs, saying; “Show me what you’ve got, boy!”

Wolf smiled down at me, saying; “Yes, Sir!” He reached up with both hands to lift his hair up, letting it slowly, sensuously cascade down over his broad shoulders and thick chest like a shiny black waterfall. Wolf knew how much I loved the look and feel of, and how much I was turned on by his luxuriant ebony mane. That was one of the reasons he spent as much time taking care of his hair as he did. He had also told me that it was an important part of his Native American heritage, but I secretly thought that his hair turned him on as well.

When his hair had fallen, Wolf slowly tilted up his head, shaking his hair back, so his chest was bare, his hair flowing down over his back. He slowly and erotically stroked his fingers lightly over his chest while sensuously licking his lips with a teasing expression on his face. Wolf was proud of his muscles, damned proud; he loved showing them off for me almost as much as he loved worshiping my muscles. I knew in his heart he was a bit of an exhibitionist, he loved to show off by being tortured at the bars in the city.

He started to play with his still swollen nipples, pulling and squeezing them. With his eyes closed he moaned softly in ecstasy. His abs rippled as he flexed his muscles, deep breaths expanding his chest for my benefit.

As he worked his bulging muscles, sweat started to bead up on his chest, running in small trickling streams down his sculpted torso, over his ribs and down onto his abs. He sensuously began to slowly rub the sweat shining on his skin, stroking his gleaming muscles, while I watched.

He raised his arms up into a double bicep pose, his muscles and veins bulging under his bronze skin, small trickles of sweat trickling down from his deep armpits to run down his ribcage on each side of his torso. I panted with pleasure and lust when he turned his head to one side, to delicately lick his right bicep. I loved watching his pink tongue flicking over as much of his arm as he could reach, tracing the thick arteries that coursed along the length of his muscled arm, licking up his own sweat. With his left hand, he reached down to stroke his glistening, hairless pecs and abs, playing with his nipples. Wolf turned his head to repeat the erotic show for me with his other arm. The entire time, his cock stood out from his crotch, erect, dripping, and throbbing over my chest.

Wolf continued his incredibly erotic showing off of his sculpted physique for me for almost ten minutes, including using his fingers to outline each groove of his ripped, washboard abdominal muscles. He would rub one hand over his sweat-glazed body, from his broad shoulders all the way down to his vascular, ripped thighs. He licked his sweat from his fingers, sucking each finger into his hot mouth, moaning with pleasure the entire time, while the other hand continued his self-torture of his nipples. His hips grinding against my rock hard cock teased it, causing me to moan in almost uncontrollable lust as I watched him make love to his own body.

When I couldn't resist any longer, I reached out, wrapping my hands around the cheeks of Wolf's hard ass, slowly pulling him towards me, sliding him up my abs and chest until I could stretch out my tongue to tease the head of his cock. Wolf growled in unbridled lust as my tongue played over the head of his swollen, throbbing cock. I kept pulling him closer to my face, until I could suck most of the length of his shaft into my mouth.

He groaned, "Oh Fuck, Sir!" as I began to play with his nipples as I sucked his cock.

I sucked him for just a few minutes, as I didn't want him to cum just yet. I had another plan to get Wolf off. Finally, I slid him back down my abs, telling him; "O.K. boy, now it's time for you to service your master!"

He lay down on top of me, his sweat-slick body sliding across my chest, kissing me deeply as his hair flowed down to enclose both our faces. He slowly traced his way down my face, licking and kissing my jaw line, under my chin and down my neck. His tongue ran over my sweat glazed pecs, flicking my nipples and licking out my armpits. Slowly he worked his way down over my ribcage to my abs, all the while stroking my sides with his hands. The combination of sensations, hot mouth, light fingers; combined with the silky-soft brush of his hair and the warmth of his hard, sweat drenched muscled body on my skin, was incredibly erotic. Eyes closed, I lay back with my hands under my head again, lost in the unbelievably sensuous feeling of Wolf worshiping my muscles, listening to the wordless song of Wolf's soft moans while he made love to my body.

Tracing my abs for a while, he outlined each muscle of my six-pack with his tongue, nibbling on each cord of hard, defined muscle while playing with my nipple rings with his strong hands. He stuck his tongue deeply into my navel, causing me to groan in pure ecstasy.

Wolf descended to my erect, throbbing cock, his hot breath feeling like a blowtorch on my sensitive shaft, the feel of his tongue flicking lightly across my cockhead and gently down the length of my dick was almost beyond description. I moaned with pleasure as Wolf began to lick my balls one at a time. I gasped with surprise when he sucked them both into his eager mouth. He circled them with his tongue for a few minutes before letting my nuts pop from his mouth one at a time. The feel of his soft, silky hair brushing against my cock and thighs was sheer ecstasy. He took the head of my throbbing cock between his lips, teasing, tormenting my dickhead with his teeth by nibbling gently on the incredibly sensitive skin. I groaned even louder as he slowly sucked my cock deeper into his hot mouth. I could feel his tongue tracing every vein pulsing the entire length of my cock. Over a period of months, I had trained him to take the entire nine-inch shaft deeply into his throat without the slightest hint of gagging. He kept swallowing my dick into his throat until his nose was buried in my pubic hair and his chin was against my balls. I could feel the muscles of his neck twitching as Wolf deep-throated the entire length of my rock-hard, pulsating, cock. My cock slowly emerged until only the head remained in his mouth. His tongue flickered across the tip of my cock while his lips encased the shaft, his teeth nibbling gently on my tender skin.

I was so turned on he could only tease my cock for a minute more before I gasped, "Get ready for it, boy!"

Wolf lowered his mouth all the way back down on my cock, twisting and pulling on my nipples with his strong fingers just moments before I shot a hot load of cum deeply into his throat with a yell of, "Oh fuck, take it, boy! Swallow that cum, boy! Drink your master's sperm, slave!"

Wolf continued to suck me as I shot stream after stream of hot jizz into his willing mouth, only ending his relentless cocksucking and nipple work after my orgasm was totally spent.

Wolf raised his head to look at me with that lopsided grin that I loved so much. "Oh, wow, Sir, that tastes sooo good! I feel so much better now. How about you, Sir?"

I reached out my arms, pulling him down on top of my chest, saying, "Does this answer your question, boy?" Kissing him passionately, my arms encircled his muscular torso and slid up his broad back muscles. We held the kiss until I pulled my lips away from Wolf's mouth to tell him softly "I love you so much, boy! I want you to do something extra special for me today, boy."

Wolf gazed into my eyes, saying, "What's that, Sir?"

"I want you to fuck me, boy. Shove that fat cock into me! We need to see if it's completely healed and still works!" Wolf looked surprised, I had let him fuck me only a few times in the time we had been together. It was a special treat, he had to really work hard to earn it!

"Oh yes, Sir. Thank you, Sir" he said, reaching for the lube I kept in the nightstand next to the bed. In moments he had his thick eight-inch cock shiny with lube. Kneeling between my legs, he lifted them up to spread them apart, exposing my ass. He used his fingers to apply lube to my asshole, then slowly probed the fat head of his dick inside me. I gasped at the feel of the intrusion, the brief pain rapidly turning into a feeling of almost unbearable pleasure. Wolf gradually drove himself inside me, going slightly deeper with each thrust until the entire length of his shaft was buried in my ass. He slowly worked himself in and out of my ass for a couple of minutes, teasing me, allowing me to get used to having his thick cock buried inside me. Now I knew I was ready for a good stiff fuck.

"Okay, boy, fuck me. Fuck me hard and deep, boy!" I growled at him.

Wolf began pumping in and out of my ass harder, faster, his cock sliding in and out of my tight hole. The sweat glistened on his bronzed torso, as every muscle in his body rippled and flexed under his skin. I reached out to grasp his still tender nipples, squeezing and twisting them, I knew that this would drive him nuts while he fucked me.

Wolf growled and began slamming his cock into me even harder as I worked on his tits. He fucked my ass thoroughly, alternating between a fierce pounding of my hole, and a slower, but still hard driving of his entire shaft into me, as he worked himself close to an orgasm before pausing to cool down a bit.

At last Wolf started pounding his cock in and out of me like some kind of frenzied, rutting beast in the throes of a primal mating frenzy, the sweat streaming down his bulging pecs and washboard abs, dripping from his magnificently muscled body onto my skin as he ravaged my willing ass. His stomach rippled like the surface of a storm-tossed ocean of muscle with each thrust of his thick cock into my hole. His eyes were closed with an expression of total raw animal lust on his face. The veins bulged under the skin of his rock hard biceps and forearms as he held my legs spread wide, giving him the look of the victim of a crucifixion struggling against his bondage, as every muscle in his incredible physique was flexing under his skin. His hair was plastered to his chest and shoulders by his sweat, adding to his wild man looks. I gave myself in to the sensations ripping through my entire body from my stretched asshole, hollering at Wolf to "Fuck me, boy! Drive that cock into your master's ass, boy!"

The harder I yanked and twisted on his huge nipples, the harder and more intensely he fucked me, his balls slapping wetly against my ass. He grunted and growled with each thrust of his swollen, engorged cock into my willing hole.

After what seemed to be an eternity to my endorphin overloaded mind, but was actually only a few more minutes, Wolf panted "I'm gonna cum, Sir! Oh God, I'm gonna shoot!"

"Do it, boy," I groaned, "Shoot that hot load on me!"

Wolf pulled his cock out of my ass, pumping it furiously with his hand. Within seconds, he threw his head back and with a deep-throated; "OH FUCK! OH FUCK!" shot a huge load of cum across my torso. It seemed to be even bigger than the load he had shot on the rack the night before. As he shot, I twisted his nipples as hard as I could, adding to his orgasm. Wolf grunted and growled in his throat until the cum finally stopped shooting from his dick, then, slumping forward, he lowered his head and began licking his load from my body. I lay there, my chest heaving and my breath laboring in my throat from the unbelievably erotic feeling of having had Wolf's thick cock inside me and now feeling his hot tongue on my body.

I let him lick me clean and then pulled him down on top of me again, our bodies' seal-slick from the hot sweat coating both of us. I could feel the pounding of both of our hearts slamming in our chests.

"Thank you, boy, that was great! I guess we proved that your cock still works." I grinned at him, then kissed him deeply again. I could taste the remnants of our semen in his mouth. When I released him from the kiss, I looked deeply into his eyes to tell him "I have another surprise for you this morning, boy."

Wolf's eyes widened slightly as he said "Another one, Sir? I thought fucking you was as big a surprise as I could ask for, Sir!"

"I think you will like this one as well, boy. We have been invited to visit a friend's leather ranch next week, boy."

Wolf looked slightly uncertain as he asked "A leather ranch, Sir?"

I smiled. "It used to be a working cattle ranch, but now it's like a tourist dude ranch in the country, but everyone there is a gay guy into leather. The guy who owns it used to be a semi-regular fuck-buddy and sometime slave of mine, until he bought the property from an uncle who wanted to retire, then moved out there full time with his lover. According to the description he e-mailed me, there are private guest cabins, bunkhouses for orgies, a slave training facility, lots of space for outdoor bondage scenes, a barn for a torture chamber and things like that. You'll need to figure out what kind of outdoor bondage and torture scenes you might like to endure while we're there, because we'll be able to do a lot of things there we just can't do in the city. I have to admit it sounds like 'A really wholesome, fun place for the whole family!'"

I deepened my voice to my "TV announcer guy" voice on the last line, causing Wolf to laugh out loud.

"Sounds great, Sir. I already know at least one thing I want done to me while we're there! When do we leave?" He was grinning from ear to ear.

"How soon can you pack, boy?" I was smiling, too because Wolf's enthusiasm was infectious.

"I can be ready in a half hour, if you want, Sir" Wolf started to climb out of bed, but I grabbed him and pulled him back

"Whoa there boy," I told him laughing, "We don't leave for a few days so there's no hurry. We have to figure exactly what to take with us and all the other little things, like which car from the collection to use, and I have to get exact directions, so there is no reason to run off half cocked."

Wolf slyly reached down between my legs and said "I never would think of you as half cocked, Sir. If that's only half, I would really hate to see the whole thing, Sir!"

That was another thing I loved so much about my handsome slave boy-lover. He knew when to be serious, like when we were out in public at a bar or during a scene, but he also knew when he could be silly with me, usually when we were alone, which was fun, because Wolf's sense of humor was almost as twisted, irreverent, and totally whacked out as mine was.

He also knew when he could relax some of our rules of conduct, like being able to speak without permission, and when he had to obey them strictly. That was part of his training as my slave and part of his freedom as my lover.

I smiled up at him and said, "How about some breakfast, boy?" Then looking at the clock on the nightstand I told him "Better make that lunch!"

As Wolf got up out of bed, he suddenly bent over slightly and groaned.

"What's the matter, boy?" I asked him.

"God, my back aches, Sir" he replied.

"Well, I guess fucking someone like a madman after being stretched a full six inches on the rack would tend to hurt the next day, boy" I told him with a smirking look on my face.

"Ha-Ha. Very funny, Sir. You need to try it sometime and see how it feels." He grumped a bit, slowly straightening up with a groan.

I looked at him and told him in all seriousness "I have, boy. I have never done anything to you, with one exception, that I haven't had done to me at one time or another. Every torture you've ever endured, with the exception of your burning, I've also had to endure. How do you think I know just how hard to work that hot body of yours to hurt you the most, boy? "

Wolf looked startled. "You're serious, right? I can't see you as a bottom boy or someone's slave, Sir. And I really have a hard time picturing you tied up and being tortured, Sir! Although now that I think of it, I bet it would be hot to see!"

"How do you think I learned to be a top, boy? I wasn't born a top man, I had to be trained. I had a master for over six years who trained me up to be a top before he passed away four years ago. He took me in when I was just twenty-two years old and had just lost my parents in a plane crash. He helped me through a really rough patch in my life, giving me a sense of direction I was missing."

Wolf was standing next to the bed, listening intently. "I never knew, Sir. I didn't mean to be a smart ass or anything like that."

I grinned up at him. "Smart ass, no. Hot ass, yes! Now go wash up and fix us something to eat. Maybe someday I'll tell you all about my sordid past." As he turned to go to the bathroom I sat up to slap him on the butt.

He turned and smiled at me. "Do you want to get started again, Sir or do you want to eat?"

I flopped back into bed and groaned, "Get going, boy before I die of starvation!"

Wolf's laughter followed him all the way from the bathroom down the stairs to the kitchen.

While waiting for Wolf to announce breakfast was ready, I reflected on the plans I had already made for our visit to the ranch, and wondered again if Wolf could endure, or even survive, the tortures I was going to subject him to. I knew what one of his ultimate outdoor torture fantasies was; I had already planned the scene. It would be part of the ultimate test of his strength and endurance. I had decided that it was time to submit Wolf to the tests to see if he was truly the slave that I wanted to have serving me for the rest of my life.

But if he could endure the tortures, the rewards I had planned for him were going to be well worth any suffering he had to endure. His life would irrevocably change, as would mine, and I knew that it would be for the better.

Chapter Five
The Ranch

Several days later, Wolf and I finished packing our car for our trip to my friend's guest ranch, which was called "The S-Bar-M." I had a special surprise hidden in the trunk of the car for Wolf, which I was going to give him if he managed to survive what I had planned for him at the ranch. We had decided to take the 1957 Chevy convertible from my car collection as I hadn't driven it for a while and it needed to be used. Since it was a hot day in early August, by the time we were on the east side of the bay, we had the top down and both of us had stripped to the waist to get a little sun on the way to the ranch. We attracted a bit of attention as some people noticed the car first, it being hard to miss a fully restored turquoise and white '57 Chevy ragtop, then they noticed Wolf and me. Wolf had woven his hair into a long braided ponytail that hung all the way down to the middle of his broad back to keep it from knotting in the wind and was wearing a red bandanna folded into a do-rag, while I wore my leather baseball cap and my mirrored shades to keep the sun out of my eyes. Wolf was sitting in the passenger seat of the Chevy, his arms spread out across the top of the seat with his head back leaving his sculpted chest stretched out for everyone to see with his thick nipples standing out from his pecs, and his ponytail draped over the back of the seat. Our deeply tanned, muscular bodies contrasted with the white leather upholstery of the Chevy; I also knew that the silver of my nipple rings stood out against the dark brown of my chest. I smiled to myself every time we got a thumbs up from truckers and other drivers or heard a wolf whistle from cars and trucks along side us on the interstate. The funny thing was that about as many waves and whistles came from other men as from women.

I said to Wolf "I wonder how many whistles are for the car, and how many are for us, boy?"

He smiled at me and said, "I don't care how many are for you or me, Sir. All I know is that I'm here in the car with you and they're not. They can look all they want, but I'm the one that will be here with you as long as you want me to be, Sir."

"Well, well, well. Aren't we being presumptuous today, boy?" I said to him, but with a wicked grin, to let him know I was teasing him. "Who knows, this weekend I might find some hot young boy to take over chief slave status at home. I hear that there's lots of hot studs on the hoof there!"

Wolf shot me a look that was so incredulous that I couldn't help breaking into delighted laughter. Seconds later, Wolf broke up too, until we were both laughing so hard I was afraid I would have to pull over and stop.

Gasping with laughter, I told him "You know that I would never try to replace you with another boy. I love you too much!" It was true, too. Some opportunities had presented themselves to me during the last year, but I always turned them down. Where could I ever hope to find a slave-boy / lover as wonderful as Wolf? Drop-dead gorgeous, totally loyal, built like a brick outhouse, long haired, and a true masochist, to boot!

We kept up the banter for the whole trip, needling and sarcastically insulting each other, as only two people who truly love each other can do, even while we stopped for lunch in a small town on the western slope of the Sierra Nevada range.

We were both amused when the young man at the drive-in window where we got a couple of burgers commented; "Whoa! Really hot, dude. And the car's great looking, too!" I just smiled at his expression of undisguised lust as I lightly ran my fingers down Wolf's chest before we pulled out of the drive-through.

When we were about five miles from the ranch, which was located near the Nevada border near the high desert north of Yosemite Park, I pulled the car to the side of the road, pulled Wolf to me, kissed him deeply, then told him that I wanted him to go into what we called "full slave mode" for the duration of our stay there, or until I told him otherwise. That involved no talking unless he was responding to a direct question from me and me only, keeping his eyes down towards the floor, not using any furniture without my specific permission; generally behaving like a totally subservient slave should. Wolf was used to this, as it was the way I insisted he behave when we went out to the bars on Folsom or in the Castro district in the city.

He agreed, saying; "That was what I had planned to do, Sir, as I don't want to embarrass you in any way while we're at your friend's place. I want everyone there to know that I have the greatest master in the world!"

I looked at him and said, "That's just another reason I love you so much, boy." I leaned over and kissed him deeply once again.

When we arrived at the ranch and pulled up to the main house to check in, I waited in my seat while Wolf jumped out and walked around to open my door for me. I got out and leaned into the back seat to pick up my vest to wear inside, plus Wolf's slave collar, which I locked on him.

"Follow me, boy," I ordered him and we entered the house; Wolf holding the door open for me. I saw my friend Chuck Wilkins, the owner of the S-bar-M behind the desk in the front room. He stood about six feet tall, with thick dark brown hair, and a work hardened, muscular, tanned body with thick biceps fairly bursting from the rolled-up sleeves of his denim work shirt.

"Well, I'll be damned! Eric, you muscle-bound son of a bitch, it's about fucking time you got here! I was starting to think you got lost!" he bellowed, in a voice you could have heard for miles out in the open. He circled around the desk, wrapped his arms around me, trying his best to squeeze the air out of my lungs. I just flexed my muscles, standing there until he gave up. I hugged him back, pulled his face to mine, and kissed him deeply, forcing my tongue deeply into his mouth, until he was squirming in my arms with pleasure. Chuck had been a fuck-buddy of mine for several years, but I hadn't seen him for over a year since he had bought the ranch from his uncle and moved from the city with his lover to live there full time. Also, he had never met Wolf before since I hadn't allowed Wolf to accompany me to the bar until I had trained him for at least three months.

"Dammit Eric, you always were the strongest bastard I ever knew," he panted, when I finally let him go.

Chuck then turned towards Wolf and said, "This must be the famous Wolfboy that I've heard about. Damn, Eric, he's a hot stud! You always had good taste!"

I glanced at Chuck, telling him "His name is Wolf, and yes, he is as hot as he looks and no, you can't have him!"

Chuck just looked at me with a wicked grin on his face, then retorted; "Oh really? I'll bet you that I get that hot ass of his at least twice while you're here!"

I snapped back; "Only in your dreams, smart-ass! If anybody is gonna get fucked while we're here, it's gonna be you!"

Chuck merely snorted derisively "HA! And who's gonna do it? You? I don't think so, pansy-boy! Your biggest muscle has always been that one between your ears! You've always been built like a brick wall, and you're about as dumb as one, too!"

Wolf, who had been standing silently, still stripped to the waist, with his eyes down during this whole exchange, gave me a brief, startled look. I caught his eye and gave him a wink. At that, Wolf looked down again, but I caught a faint glimpse of the smile he was trying to keep off his face.

"O.K. Chuck, enough bullshit, where do I sign in at this funny farm of yours? It's been a long drive and we need to clean up a bit."

He grinned at me as he went back around the desk and handed me two keys. "Cabin number four, Eric, It's the biggest one for two people and the best insulated, so no one will hear you while you abuse this poor, helpless boy of yours!"

"Abuse? Abuse?" I snapped at him in mock indignation, "I never abuse my boy. Torture him; yes, but never abuse him!"

Chuck roared with laughter. "Call it what you will, it still sounds like fun to me! I'll see you guys later; I actually have some work to do around here. I can't just lay around like some people I know!"

"Yeah, right. Bitch! Bitch! Bitch! If you didn't want the responsibilities, why'd you take over the place, then?" I shot back as we walked out to get our bags from the car.

After Wolf had carried our bags into the cabin, he said, "Permission to speak, Sir?"

"Go ahead, boy" I told him.

"I guess you have known Chuck for a while, Sir. Is he always so, er … forward, Sir?" he said hesitantly, not wanting to offend me.

I smiled. "We have an agreement to never be polite to each other until after sunset. He's also one of my oldest friends so there's nothing to worry about, boy."

Wolf smiled back. "I never worry when I'm with you, Sir."

I purposely hadn't warned Wolf about Chuck's rather outgoing personality, as I wanted to see what kind of a reaction he would get. Contrary to first appearances, Chuck was really a sweetheart of a guy, always good for lots of laughs.

I pulled my slave boy to me, giving him a big hug, then telling him to get to work cleaning my boots. Wolf obediently dropped to his knees to wipe the light coat of dust from my boots with a cloth. I would let him tongue-clean my boots later.

After Wolf had unpacked and hung up our clothes and had set up my traveling toy box for later use, we wandered around the ranch property for a bit, exploring the grounds, taking note of some of the facilities available for the guests, like the gym and pool area, the stables for horseback riding with attached corral, the bunkroom, and the barn that was the location of the main torture facilities of the ranch.

Later that evening, when we went into the main dining room for dinner, we met some of the other guests that would be at the ranch for the week or even longer. There were a few single guys, but most of the other visitors were couples, mostly master and slave duos, judging by the number of boys in collars. I could tell everyone was watching us as we walked into the dining room. I had decided to show off for the other guests there, since I figured we had put so much effort and time into developing our bodies to the level of muscularity we had, it was worth it. Also, to tell the truth, it was a real ego rush for the both of us. I had changed into a tight pair of faded jeans, my western boots, and a black cowboy hat, with a tailored, sleeveless denim shirt that showed off my biceps and triceps, while Wolf wore the same pair of cutoff shorts he was wearing the day I met him, with a black spandex muscle tank top and combat boots, along with his slave collar padlocked around his throat. He had let his hair down out of the braided ponytail so it flowed over his chest and shoulders and down his back from under the red bandanna, which he had rolled and was wearing as a headband. I figured the Cowboys-and-Indians contrast in our appearances would feed some of the fantasies of some of the guys. I could see from some of the looks that we were getting from some of the hot men and boys there that we would definitely be having a good time at the ranch this week.

I decided to show off Wolf's training a little bit, so I deliberately took a seat at the end of a table, so Wolf would have to kneel on the floor next to my seat. When I sat down, I merely snapped my fingers and pointed to the floor next to me. Wolf immediately dropped to his knees, his hands crossed behind his back, with his head down and his eyes on the floor. I heard a murmur of comments from some of the other guys in the dining room, but kept a straight face and merely ordered for the both of us.

When our food arrived, I told Wolf he had my permission to use the utensils to eat and he could put his plate on the table to eat, but had to eat while kneeling, as I hadn't given him permission to use any furniture yet. He answered, "Thank you, Master" and began eating.

I knew that he understood what I was doing because he didn't call me "Master" unless we were in a special situation; normally he called me "Sir." It was one of the little ways we had of communicating our thoughts to each other without anyone else catching on.

After we were done with dinner, we went into the main living room / lobby to visit with some of the other guests and relax a bit from our drive before starting any activities for the night. I sat in one of the easy chairs with Wolf kneeling next to me, leaning against my leg, nuzzling my thigh, while I stroked his silky hair. As we were relaxing and casually chatting with various other guests, including getting our first open propositions for sex, the first compliments on both my looks and muscles, and on my slave boy and how well he was trained, a young, lean but muscular blonde boy with a collar approached my chair, knelt in front of me and said, “May I have permission to speak to you, Sir?”

“Go ahead” I told him.

“My master’s compliments, Sir. He would like to know if you and your handsome slave would like to join us for a drink in the lounge, Sir.”

“Tell your master we would be delighted to and we will be there in about five minutes, boy, after we visit the restroom. Now go give him my answer, boy.”

“Yes, Sir. Thank you, Sir.” He rose to turn, headed back across the lobby into the lounge, which was in a small room off the side of the main room.

I squeezed Wolf’s shoulder telling him “Come on, boy” as I got to my feet. He stood up and silently followed me into the restroom. After I relieved myself of some of the water I had drunk on the drive up to the ranch, seeing that there was no one else there, I asked Wolf; “So, what do you think so far, boy? You have permission to speak to me when we are alone, boy.”

He turned towards me with a huge smile on his face and said, “I think I’m going to like it here, Sir. Thank you for bringing me!”

I gave him a big hug and said, “Well, who else was I going to bring, you big lummox? Now let’s go meet these guys and see what kind of trouble we can get into!”

We went out into the lobby, across to the lounge where the blonde boy immediately met us, and led us over to a table in the corner to meet his master, who stood up as we approached his table. He was a tall, muscular, bearded man named Donald, with a coat of shiny black hair covering his sculpted chest and abs, visible under his open shirt. He introduced us to his boy, whose name was Jason, but was normally known as just Jay. I introduced myself to them, then introduced Wolf, telling him to give a proper greeting to another master. He dropped to his knees and bowed down, pressing his forehead to the tops of Donald’s boots. Wolf then sat back up on his haunches and I started stroking his hair again. I heard Jay give a quiet “Wow” of either admiration or awe. His master turned to him, saying; “Now that’s the way a properly trained bottom is supposed to behave, boy. You noticed that he didn’t kiss or lick my boots. That honor is reserved for his master exclusively, unless ordered otherwise. When will you learn to do that, boy?”

Jay softly answered; “I’m sorry, Master. I’ve never seen anyone do that before. I didn’t know about that rule, Sir, but I’ll remember it from now on,

Sir."

Donald turned to me, apologizing; "I've only had him about a month, he's my first slave, and we are both still learning. But I have hopes for him."

I smiled at both of them; "There's no need to apologize. The first thing to remember is that no one is born a slave, and no one is born a master. Both need to be trained. Sometimes it just takes a while to change a slave boy's way of thinking. Just keep at him and eventually he'll come around and start acting properly. I've owned Wolf for over a year and I still have to discipline him every so often when he slips up."

I turned to Wolf, giving him a wink, and said, "Don't I, boy?"

Wolf just blushed slightly and softly answered, "Yes, Sir."

We sat in the lounge for about an hour or so, drinking a couple of soft drinks, discussing various aspects of the Master and Slave lifestyle from both sides, as I gave Wolf permission to speak to be able to answer questions from both Don and Jay. We talked about things like the difference between an S&M scene and real torture and how to recognize the line between pleasure and pain.

Donald was 28 and a first time master, while Jay was only 22, a novice slave, in his first relationship of any kind since leaving his home. I was relieved to hear that Donald had been in a relationship as a slave, and still liked to be a bottom occasionally, as I truly believed that the only way to truly be a good top was to have been a bottom first. They were from the Denver area and were visiting the ranch for the first time, just like Wolf and I. It was also fun to be able to find out how things were going at my favorite bar in Denver, The Triangle. I hadn't had an opportunity to visit it for a while and I was relieved to hear that it was just as hot as ever.

We also had a discussion on proper slave training, behavior, and most importantly, an outline on how to communicate during a scene, both verbally with safe words, and non-verbally, using pre-arranged gestures or other signals to alert the top that his slave was in excess discomfort. S&M scenes are supposed to be fun, not dangerous to either party.

Finally, I stood up and told Wolf to get up off his knees. He did so a little stiffly, as he had been kneeling the entire time. I told Donald and Jay we would probably see them in the barn a little later that night, as I planned to show off Wolf a little bit, subjecting him to a heavy session of painful discipline and good old fashioned torture.

We went back to our cabin to change for the night. When we were done I asked Wolf "Well boy, are you ready to show what you can take tonight? I intend to take you right to the edge, boy!"

Wolf smiled as he dropped to his knees in front of me, leaning down to kiss my polished boots. He straightened back up and softly said, “Yes, Sir. I will take whatever you want to do to me, Sir. You know that I love it when you torture me, Sir. I want to make you as proud of my being your slave as I am proud that you are my Master, Sir.”

I gazed down into his deep brown eyes, seeing the love and respect there, as a single tear rolled down his right cheek. As he knelt in front of me, stripped to the waist, I admired his handsome, sculpted face, framed by his thick mane of luxuriant black hair, realizing that Wolf had never appeared more totally, absolutely beautiful to me than he did at this moment. He was almost heartbreakingly handsome. I realized at that moment I had been blessed with this young man, who out of everyone in the city, had chosen to give himself to me, had chosen to allow me to use him however I wanted to. As I began to feel the absurd sting of tears of happiness and gratitude building behind my own eyes, I told Wolf to stand up. I wrapped my arms around his hard, sculpted physique to pull him to my chest. No other words were necessary as we held each other close for a minute. I loved the feel of his warm skin pressed to my chest, his hair flowing down over both our shoulders. As he leaned his face down between my pecs, I felt several more tears fall from my slave’s eyes to drop on my skin.

Finally I pulled back from his embrace, kissed him deeply on his full lips and said “O.K., boy, let’s go to the barn and show these other guys what the best slave here is able to take from his master!”

Wolf smiled at me and said “Yes, Sir! That’ll be easy, Sir. I’ve got the best master here!”

I told him to pick up my toy box and follow me. Wearing only his cutoffs and boots, with his hair flowing down over his chest and shoulders, his leash attached to the collar locked firmly around his throat, Wolf grabbed my box, and turned to follow me, his muscles rippling under his brown skin. I knew we were going to have a good time that night and over the next few days, no matter what. I already had some surprises planned for Wolf, including exploring part of his Native American heritage, by forcing him to endure some brutally painful Indian inspired tortures that would test him to the very limits of his physical strength, as well as taking him to the edge of his ability to endure pain. I had planned, when I received Chuck’s invitation, that this week was going to be the make-or-break point of my relationship with Wolf. If he survived the week, he would be mine forever.

Chapter Six
Training

I led Wolf on the end of his leash into the barn where the main torture chamber had been set up at the ranch. There was an impressive amount of equipment set up for the guests to use, including several St. Andrew's crosses and upright crucifixion crosses, both horizontal and vertical racks, suspension harnesses, slings and other bondage and torture devices including a couple of old jail cell doors fastened at an angle to one wall of the barn.

After looking around the barn for a few minutes and seeing the huge assortment of dungeon equipment available, I led Wolf over to one side of the main room to where two vertical beams with chains, hooks, eyebolts and electric winches were located. Telling Wolf to set my toy box down, I unclipped the leash from his collar, gathered him in my arms and whispered in his ear; "Whatever I do to you tonight, I do it because I love you and I want you to be happy."

He smiled, softly saying, "Yes, Sir, Thank you Sir, I love you, too and will take whatever you do to me because it will make you happy, too, Sir"

I released him and instructed him to strip off his shorts, leaving him wearing only his combat boots and white socks and his collar. When he had done so, I fastened padded restraints around his wrists and ankles. I positioned him between the beams and attached the chains leading from the winches to his wrist restraints. Spreading his feet, I hooked short lengths of chain to his ankles and, using the controls for the electric winches, began to pull his arms up and over his head until he was standing in a tightly stretched spread-eagled position.

I observed that we were already beginning to draw a group of guys watching to see what I was going to do to my handsome slave. Seeing this, I asked Wolf loudly, "Are you ready, boy? Do you want it? You have my permission to answer, boy!"

"Oh yes, Sir, please!" he answered, knowing exactly what I was doing, playing to the crowd.

I used the controls for the winches to draw the chains on his arms tighter until, with a groan, Wolf lifted off of the floor. I kept the winches running until the chains attaching Wolf's ankles to the eyebolts at the base of the beams drew taut, stretching his entire body. Wolf groaned again as he was pulled tighter and tighter, until he was stretched so tightly he was having a hard time drawing a deep breath as his diaphragm was strained by the weight of his body.

I stripped off my vest and went up to my suspended slave, admiring the planes of his muscles and ribcage, rippling and bulging under his bronze skin. His cock was already swollen and throbbing gently, showing his willingness to accept whatever torture I wanted to inflict on him. I stroked my fingers down his ribcage and twisted, pulled and chewed on his tits. Moving behind him, I brushed his hair forward over his shoulders and stroked the rock hard, straining muscles bunched under the tanned skin of his v-tapered back, his broad shoulders, and his thick upper arms. I could hear an excited murmuring coming from the group of onlookers watching and awaiting Wolf's imminent torture.

I turned and reached into my toy box and brought out my lightweight flogger, the one I liked to use to warm up his back to get it ready for heavier whipping later in a scene. Wolf moaned softly as I started to lightly use the flogger on his broad shoulders and heavily muscled back, slowly working my way down to his rounded ass. The skin on his back began to shine with a sheen of sweat even as it started turning a deeper red as I increased the intensity of his flogging.

I worked on him for about five minutes with the light flogger before I started working my way through several more floggers over the next ten minutes or so up to my heaviest, a braided cat made of buffalo hide. I had to work this cat carefully, because it was fully capable of cutting into skin and leaving bloody welts. I slowly worked the intensity up until Wolf was twisting and straining in his bonds with each impact of the cat. He was trying to remain silent, as I had not given him permission to speak since answering my question, but it was harder and harder for him to be quiet as the intensity and the pain level of the flogging increased.

Finally I told him, while continuing to whip him, "O.K. boy, let it out."

He gasped a strangled sounding "Thank you, Sir", and then gave a sharp cry at each impact of the cat on his tortured flesh. I continued to flog him for about another ten minutes, at the end of which, Wolf's back was a deep angry red color, crossed with lines of welts raising on his flesh.

I put the flogger back in the toy box and went around to face my battered slave. He hung in the chains, tightly stretched, moaning softly and gasping for breath, his head slumped forward with his chin on his chest, his sweat-streaked chest rising and falling with each labored breath.

"Was that a good start, boy?" I asked him harshly, lifting his chin so he was looking into my eyes. "Do you want more, boy?"

"Yes, Sir, please, Sir" he answered. "Whatever you want to do to me, Sir

"Good, boy, because we are just getting started!" I snarled at him loudly, so all the other men watching would hear. I heard a low moan come from the group.

I brushed Wolf's hair back so it was hanging down his back and, going back to the toy box, picked up the lightweight flogger again and proceeded to repeat the entire increasing intensity flogging on his tightly stretched and straining chest, stomach, and thighs! By the time I was done, Wolf was screaming in agony with each impact of the heavy flogger on his striped, welted body, his head thrown back, his eyes closed, and tears running down his cheeks.

Putting the flogger back, I stepped up to Wolf and, grabbing a handful of his hair, pulled his head forward so I could look directly into his eyes. I wanted to check him to be sure he was capable of continuing the scene safely. The last thing I would ever want to do would be to injure my slave just to show off in a scene.

Softly I asked him, "Are you still with me, boy? Do you want to continue?"

His eyes focused on me and he whispered "Yes, Sir. I want more."

I smiled at him and was a bit surprised to see Wolf weakly smile back and give me a wink of his eye. I knew then that he was all right and really wanted more and wasn't just showing off for the other guys watching.

Stepping back, I turned to look at the group of about a dozen guys watching us and was amused to see at least seven or eight of them had their cocks out and were stroking them. A few even had their slave boys down sucking them while they watched. I saw Donald and his boy Jay and motioned for them to come closer.

"Do you still think he needs more discipline?" I asked Donald, referring to what he had told me about Jay earlier in the day.

Donald answered "Yes, Master Eric. He does, but I'm not sure how to give it to him. He is my first slave and I'm still learning. Would you show me, please Sir? My boy is yours to command, Sir."

Turning to Jay, I told him to strip down to his boots and his collar. As he did, I went to my toy box and searched briefly for the equipment needed to set up the scene that I was even then working out in my head. When I turned back to them, Jay was standing there with his hands crossed behind his back and his head down in a classic posture of submission.

"Well, he seems to have some discipline already," I told Donald.

"He does, but he can't maintain it for long." Donald answered.

I could see Jay's face slowly turning redder as we discussed him as if he wasn't there listening to our every word.

I ordered Jay to hold out his arms while I fastened restraints around his wrists. I told him to look directly up into my eyes.

"Do you want to serve me, boy?" I asked him. "Your master has given you to me to use any way I want. I will not injure you, but you will be hurting when we're done, just so you know. If you don't think you are ready to endure my torture, tell me now. I'll understand, but don't say you want me to work on you, and then wimp out on me five minutes later!"

He answered softly "Yes, Sir. I will do my best, Sir, to endure whatever you want to do to me."

I pulled his face to my sweat-glazed chest and told Jay to suck on my hard tits. I let him worship my nipples and my pecs for a few minutes until I growled at him; "I think you're having too much fun. Now it's time for you to serve my slave, boy!"

I reminded them about my safe words and gestures to use when a scene was too intense to continue. I told both of them, "It's not a problem to use safe words in a scene. It's more of a problem if you don't use them and someone ends up getting injured. Remember, a scene is supposed to be pleasurable for everyone involved."

We turned towards Wolf who still hung in his chains recovering from the extreme total body flogging I had given him. He groaned as I tied a length of leather thong tightly around his balls, leaving about two feet hanging on each end. He then sucked his breath in pain as I clipped the exquisitely painful nylon crocodile clips on his thick nipples.

I told Jay; "Boy, you said earlier today that you thought my slave was handsome. Do you want to suck his cock?"

Jay answered; "Yes, Sir. I would love to suck him if you would let me, Sir."

"Good, because that's exactly what you are going to do. On your knees in front of him, boy!"

Jay immediately knelt in front of Wolf and started to lean in to take Wolf's dick into his mouth.

I grabbed a handful of his hair and, yanking him back, snarled; "Did I give you permission to do that, boy? I said on your knees and that's all, boy!"

He softly answered; “No, Sir. I’m sorry, Sir.”

“All right, boy, since you are a new slave, I will give you one mistake. That was it. The next one will cost you. Is that understood, boy?” I growled at him.

“Yes, Sir. I understand, Sir.”

“O.K. boy, now you can take Wolf’s cock into your mouth, but just hold it there, no sucking on it or any tongue work, boy. Understood, boy?”

Jay softly said; “Yes, Sir” and leaned in and slid his mouth over Wolf’s swollen cock. Wolf groaned at the feel of the hot mouth engulfing his dick. I knelt down next to Jay and, gathering up the thongs hanging from my slave’s balls, wrapped them several times tightly around Jay’s throat above his collar and then tied the ends together behind his neck so he could not pull his head back far enough to get Wolf’s cock out of his mouth. I stood up and told Jay to raise his hands straight over his head. When he did, I took his right wrist and fastened the d-ring on the restraint to the ring hanging from Wolf’s nipple clamp on that side. I did the same for his other wrist, leaving Jay on his knees in front of my suspended slave, with Wolf’s thick cock filling his mouth with no way for Jay to get it out, and his arms stretched over his head fastened to Wolf’s tits.

“Now, boy, we are going to see just how much self-discipline you really have!” I told him. “If you hurt my slave by pulling too hard on his tits or biting his cock, there will be hell to pay, boy!”

Jay could only make a muffled “mmpf” as I reached around his lean torso and began to squeeze and twist his nipples, causing him to squirm and strain, while trying to keep his hands still to avoid pulling Wolf’s nipples. He moaned even louder when I fastened a pair of my medium pressure tit clamps on his chest.

Donald looked at his slave being forced to control his every move and said; “God, Master Eric, that’s hot! I didn’t think he could control himself that well!”

I stood up and told Donald; “This is nothing. I haven’t even started to work on him yet!”

I said it loudly enough so Jay could not possibly miss hearing me, while at the same time I gave Donald a wink to let him know that I wasn’t going to hurt his boy. Donald grinned at me to let me know he understood. I then picked up my lightest flogger and, brushing it across Jay’s back, said; “Now let’s see just how much self control he really has.”

Donald said, “I think you should know, Master Eric, that my slave is not used to being whipped or flogged. I don’t know how to do it that well, and I don't want to injure him."

I told him, "Thanks for telling me that so I will know how hard to work him. Just watch and you will get a little insight into whipping without injury. If you want, I'll let you practice later on Wolf!" I grinned a little at the questioning look Wolf shot me at that! I winked at him and saw the ghost of a grin teasing the corners of his mouth as he realized I was having a bit of fun at his expense.

Jay stiffened and the muscles in his lean torso began to flex as I began to work the cat lightly across his back. I flogged him lightly for about five minutes until I told him; "All right, boy this is what is going to happen. You can start to work Wolf's cock to get him off, but you will have to take his load down your throat. The faster you can get him off, the sooner I will release you, but if you are thinking of deliberately sucking his cock slowly and taking too long to get him off, just remember I will be increasing the level of your flogging. The longer it takes you to get him off, the more intense your flogging will be. Also, remember where your hands are fastened, and what I said earlier. Hurt Wolf's tits and you will get a first hand lesson in what it means to be tortured for real! Is that understood, boy?"

Jay's only response was another muffled grunt, and then he began to work Wolf's cock as well as he could. I continued to lightly lay the tails of the cat across Jay's back for another minute or two, but then began to slowly increase the force of each stroke. Wolf groaned in his restraints as Jay increased the level of his cocksucking as the impacts on his back began to get stronger and stronger. Wolf then let out a yelp of pain as Jay flinched involuntarily, causing the clamps to stretch his already tender nipples.

"O.K. boy, what did I tell you about hurting my slave? That is going to cost you at least fifteen minutes of extra torture, boy!" I snarled down to Jay as I laid the tails of the cat across his shoulders even harder. Jay visibly struggled to control his movements as I continued to flog him. He was such a fair-skinned blonde that the flogging was starting to leave angry looking red stripes across his lean back, even though I wasn't using much force in his flogging, compared to the way I could work Wolf! Tears were running down his face as he continued to work on Wolf's swollen cock with his mouth.

The scene continued for another few minutes until Wolf began to gasp and grunt in the way that I knew meant that he was on the brink of an orgasm. I looked into his eyes and told him; "Go ahead, boy, fill that cocksucking slave's mouth with your load! Shoot it into him, boy, make him swallow your sperm!"

Wolf threw his head back and howled as his muscles rippled and bulged as he shot a thick, hot load of cum into Jay's throat. Jay coughed and sputtered as he tried to swallow the man juice filling his mouth. As he struggled to swallow it all, I reached down and unfastened the tit clamps from Jay's nipples, twisting and stretching his tits, causing him to moan and struggle even harder. The muscles in his lean, wiry back flexed with the strain of trying to control his movements even as I tortured his nipples.

Finally I released Jay's tits and untied the thongs from around his throat, allowing him to let Wolf's softening cock out of his mouth. He gasped for air but remembered to keep his arms stretched tightly over his head until I released his wrist restraints from Wolf's nipple clamps. I then told Jay "Stand up, boy."

He rose to his feet in front of me and stood with his eyes down as I fastened his hands together behind his back, his body streaked with sweat and his cock standing out hard in front of him. I turned to Donald and said, "Well, what do you think now. Is there hope for him?"

Donald just smiled and shook his head as he said; "God, Master Eric, I wouldn't have thought he could do that! That was amazing!"

I looked at Jay as I told him; "Oh, we're not done yet, not by a long shot!" I then told Jay to face Wolf as he hung in his chains.

"Does he turn you on, boy, all those muscles and that hair and everything, boy?"

"Oh yes, Sir, he is gorgeous. As are you, too." He added hastily.

"All right, if you think he is so good looking, then get that face into those armpits and start licking until I tell you that you can stop. I want you to clean every drop of slave sweat out of those pits, boy. Now get to work!"

Jay immediately leaned in and buried his face in Wolf's left armpit. Wolf groaned loudly as Jay's hot mouth began sucking and chewing on his pit. Wolf then howled even louder as I unclipped the tit clamp from his right nipple, causing him to flex and strain his muscles which made his armpit go deeper, making Jay bury his face even deeper into the pit. I allowed Jay to lick out Wolf's left pit for a few minutes before I ordered him to switch sides and clean out the right armpit. I unfastened the clamp from Wolf's other tit, causing him to howl and strain again, forcing Jay to struggle to lick the deep armpit.

After a few minutes, I snarled to Jay; "OK boy, I want you to clean all the sweat off of my slave's chest and abs! Get to work!"

Jay immediately started licking Wolf's stretched torso from the base of his neck all the way down to his crotch, running his tongue over Wolf's rippling ribs, his washboard abs, and everywhere else he could reach for another five minutes or so.

Finally, I grabbed Jay's hair and pulled him back from my suspended slave. I turned his face towards me and snarled at him; "O.K. boy, that's enough for now. I think you are enjoying yourself entirely too much!"

I turned towards Donald and asked him; "Do you want to discipline your boy or do you want me to do it for you?"

He thought for a few seconds before answering, "I think I want to do it myself, Master Eric. Thank you for showing me how much he can take. It will be interesting to see if I can manage to take him right to the edge myself."

I grinned at him and told him "Have fun. The best way to really bond with a boy is to work him hard, but always remember that anything you do to him is best done with love."

I told Jay to stand still while I removed the restraints from his wrists.

Donald then said to Jay, "Lets see if you learned anything yet. How would you thank Master Eric for your lesson and the use of his handsome slave, boy?"

Jay immediately dropped to his knees in front of me and, bending down, began to lick my boots.

I looked at Donald and said, "I guess he's starting to learn a little. Any slave has to start somewhere. I think with a little training, he will be a really good slave."

Donald said, "Thank you, Master Eric. Coming from you, that means a lot to me and to my boy." Then he told Jay, "O.K. boy, that's enough. We have to go and continue your lesson in private, and I think Master Eric wants to be with his slave for a while."

Jay rose to his feet and stood with his head bowed while I gave Donald a hug and told him if he had any questions to feel free to ask. He thanked me and led his boy off to another corner of the dungeon barn.

I turned back to Wolf, who hung in the chains between the pillars, silently watching the breaking in of what I hoped would eventually be a good slave boy. I stepped up to him and, grasping his chin in my hand, forcing him to look directly into my eyes, asked him "Is that enough for tonight, boy or do you want more? I will let you decide, boy!"

Wolf softly said, "I think I want to be alone with you, if that is all right with you, Sir."

"All right, boy, we'll go back to the cabin. But don't think that we're done for the night, boy!" I added for the benefit of the guys still watching us.

"Yes, Sir. Thank you, Sir!"

I operated the controls on the winches, slowly lowering Wolf back down to the floor of the barn and then released him from the chains where he had been suspended, hanging by his arms for over an hour. He groaned softly as I slowly lowered his arms down to his sides to prevent muscle cramps caused by dropping his arms too swiftly.

"Come here, boy." I softly told him, and wrapped my arms around him to support him. As I held my trembling slave, we were both surprised to hear the sound of applause coming from the group of men watching the scene.

Holding Wolf tightly, I whispered into his ear "They like us. They really, really like us!"

I immediately heard a muffled snort and then felt Wolf's body shaking with the effort to not laugh out loud in front of the other guys.

Finally I decided to show a little mercy to Wolf and turned to the men around us. "I guess I need to get my boy back to our cabin so he can rest. It's been a long day." Then to Wolf I said, "Get my toy box, boy."

Wolf collected my equipment and packed it up and then hoisting my toy box, followed me back to the cabin. Just as soon as the door closed behind him, Wolf burst out laughing from my quip.

"Oh, you son-of-a-bitch!" he gasped, howling with laughter. "Do you know how hard I had to work to keep a straight face?"

I grinned at him. "If you have a straight face, it's the only thing about you that IS straight!"

I couldn't help it then and started laughing as well. Within minutes we both were helpless with laughter. Sometimes that was the reaction we would have to a really hot scene. I suppose it had to do with endorphin release or something, but occasionally it just happened, and when it did, there wasn't a thing either one of us could do about it except just enjoy it.

After a few minutes we both calmed down enough to be able to sit together and relax after the scene. Finally I asked Wolf, "Do you want to grab a shower and go to bed now, boy? It has been a long day, after all. And just think, it's just our first day here. We have a whole week to play."

"Oh God" groaned Wolf, in his best hopeless martyr tone. "I don't think I'll survive! Please, just put me out of my misery now, Sir Please!"

I feigned a shocked expression. "What, and have to explain to Chuck that I wiped out my best slave in one night? Oh no, if I have to put up with him, so do you, boy!"

As we both collapsed in another helpless laughing jag before we could even get into the shower, I had the feeling that we were in for one of the best weeks that we had ever had together. And as it turned out later, I was right!

Chapter Seven
Stakeout

The next morning at breakfast I surprised Wolf by telling him in front of everyone in the dining room that I was going to give him the day off to relax and to enjoy the facilities available at the ranch. I also told him he had my permission to play if he wanted to, as long as he remained within the previously agreed to limits of acceptable behavior for a slave boy on his own.

What I didn't tell him was that I was going to use the time to prepare for his next test of endurance and pain tolerance.

After breakfast, I gave Wolf a big hug and told him to have fun during the day, that I had a few errands to take care of and that I would see him later. I knew I could trust him not to do anything out of line.

Later that afternoon, after I had returned from my errands, I asked Wolf for a review of what he had done during the day. I knew that I could trust him to be totally honest with me. He told me that he had spent a lot of the day at the pool just relaxing, as he was still a bit sore from the extreme flogging he had endured the previous night, and getting some sun, which I found to be secretly amusing, knowing what I had planned for him for the next day. He also admitted that he had sexual encounters with some of the men who had observed our scene in the barn the previous night.

I asked him for the specifics and Wolf told me that while he was lounging around the pool, two guys, who were lovers, came up to him and told him that they were amazed by what they had seen, and that they were both totally turned on by Wolf's muscles, his long hair, and his total look. They took turns worshiping his fat cock and huge nipples, and made love to his muscles, until they shared a hot load of Wolf's sperm! He also told me that he had sucked some cock and had gotten a full body massage by three guys at the same time, who all shot loads of cum on his chest and then licked him clean!

I said, "That sounds really hot, boy. But, no one fucked you, and you didn't fuck anyone else, right, boy?"

We were both disease free and I intended to keep both of us that way if at all possible.

"Yes, Sir. No one fucked me and I didn't do any fucking. I also didn't take anyone's load in my mouth. I know that's against your rules, Sir. I wouldn't do anything against the rules, Sir." Wolf looked at me with total sincerity in his eyes.

I smiled at him and told him, "That's all right, boy. I told you to have a good time and relax, and it sounds like you did. After all, we came here to have fun."

He smiled back and said, "Thank you for being understanding, Sir, and thank you for being my master, Sir." How could I not love a man like that?

Since he had been truthful with me, I told him that I had had a hard session of hot sex with one of Chuck's ranch hands, who was helping me set up my scene for the next day. He had gotten so hot by my descriptions of what I had planned for Wolf, that he had begged me to tie him up to a tree on the ranch and flog him, which I did, until he begged me to stop so he could kneel in front of me and suck me until I shot a huge load of cum down his throat.

I suggested that we should make an early night of it, as I had some interesting plans for the next day. Wolf looked mildly puzzled, and a bit disappointed, but, being the well-trained slave that he was, didn't ask any questions but merely obeyed my order. After dinner, and hanging out in the lobby for a while, chatting, we didn't go to the barn that night, but stayed in our cabin and had a session of hot, sweaty one to one man-sex that culminated with both of us swallowing a hot load of each other's cum!

The next morning, I arose and dressed early and set my plans for the day into motion with a phone call to the stables on the ranch. Minutes later there was a knock on our cabin door and when I opened it there was Jimmy, the hand I had tortured the day before, delivering a fully saddled horse with saddlebags loaded with the supplies I had packed the previous day including some of my selected toys to use on Wolf during his torture session, and my laptop.

Wolf was still bleary eyed when I told him to kneel in front of me. He immediately did as instructed and didn't say a word as I tied his hands together in front of him with a length of rope.

I then led him outside to where the horse was tied to a hitching post. Using a length of longer rope, I tied one end of it to the rope binding his wrists, and holding the other end, mounted the horse and started to head towards the area I had picked out for today's session. Wolf had no choice but to follow behind, walking totally naked in the pre-dawn chill.

We went for about a mile or so away from the main buildings of the ranch, but still on the property, until we came to a small cabin near a clearing alongside of a small river that ran through the ranch property. I untied Wolf's hands and told him to unload the supplies from the saddlebags and put them in the cabin and tie the horse to a hitching post in the shade of some trees. When he had done so, I led him out into the middle of the clearing where there were four wooden posts driven into the ground in a rectangular pattern about four feet wide by ten feet long.

Wolf's cock immediately began to swell when he figured out what I had planned for him that day. It was the fulfillment of one of his longest running fantasies. He was going to be staked-out in the sun for as long as I wanted to leave him there!

So far that morning Wolf had not said a word other than to acknowledge my orders to him, but now I asked him, "Well, boy, are you ready for this?"

He almost moaned, "Oh yes, Sir. Thank you, Sir. I've waited for this for so long, Sir!"

"Well then boy, get over here and lie down." I ordered him.

Wolf immediately lay down on the ground between the posts spreading his arms and legs as far towards the posts as he could. I took the lengths of rope that were tied at the base of two of the posts and tied one to each ankle, spreading his legs widely and exposing his cock and balls for whatever torture I wanted to inflict on them. I took the ropes on the other two posts and tied them around his wrists, stretching his arms as tightly as I could. Just as I finished tying my helpless slave boy to the posts, the sun lifted above the horizon, heralding the beginning of a day of exquisite torment for Wolf.

I leaned over my helpless slave and kissed him deeply, our tongues intertwining for as long as I held the kiss. I pulled back from him and, looking down at my slave lover, told him, "I love you so much. Do you know that, boy?"

He looked up at me and said, "Oh yes, Sir. And I love you, too, Sir!"

I leaned down and took Wolf's thick, swollen cock into my mouth, feeling the veins throbbing on the shaft. Wolf began to moan as I worked his dick deeper and deeper into my mouth. I could taste his pre-cum as I worked his cock harder and faster with my lips and tongue, and when I started to nibble on Wolf's cockhead with my teeth, he let out a growl that was his way of telling me that he was in the throes of ecstasy.

I worked Wolf's cock with my mouth for a good ten minutes until he started grunting in short growls, and the muscles of his amazing abs began to flex in a faster and faster rhythm. I leaned back and began to pump his thick shaft with my hand until, with a yell, Wolf shot his cum in thick, ropy streams all over his chest and abs.

I was so turned on by now that I stripped off my shirt, undid my belt and unbuttoned my jeans, allowing my nine-inch cock to stand out. Kneeling over my staked-out slave, I fucked his hot mouth for a while. When I was close to cumming, I pulled out of his mouth and jacked my cock until I shot on Wolf's body, my cum mixing with his load and the sweat starting to gleam on his muscles.

I grinned down at Wolf and said, "That ought to help attract the ants and other critters, boy."

He closed his eyes and softly breathed "Oh yes, Sir, I hope so, Sir!"

I got up and looked down at my helpless slave stretched tightly between the four posts, and sneered; "Don't plan on going anywhere for a while, boy. I'm gonna enjoy watching you roast!"

I then turned and silently walked back to the cabin to settle in for a long day of relaxation for me and a day of exquisite torment for Wolf. I had arranged for a supply of snacks and drinks to be delivered to the cabin and stocked in the fridge the day before, so I knew I would be comfortable while doing a few tasks on my laptop while Wolf roasted in the blazing sun. I had checked the weather forecast and was expecting a day with no clouds and temperatures in the high nineties, therefore ensuring a through roasting of my helpless slave!

Several hours passed while I worked on some essential but boring tasks on my laptop, dealing with my business investments and real estate holdings, occasionally looking out the window to check that Wolf wasn't in too much distress. I finally decided that I had done enough for a while and went out to check up personally on Wolf. He lay spread out in the sun with his eyes closed, his bronzed body glowing with sweat, his chest rising and falling in a slow rhythm.

"How are you doing, boy?" I asked, standing over him but being careful not to cast a shadow on any part of his body.

His eyes opened with a bit of a jerk, as if he had been almost asleep and had been startled by my speaking to him.

"Oh Sir, it's hot and I'm so thirsty, Sir!" he moaned. I think it may have been a bit of dramatic license for my benefit, but I decided to play along, as it helped to increase the mood of the scene.

"So you think it's hot now, do you boy?" I sneered down at Wolf. "Wait until later this afternoon when it gets close to a hundred degrees. Just think about that sun cooking your body, and think about what it will feel like when I tie you up to a tree and whip your sun burnt skin until it's raw and welted, boy!"

His only reply was a soft "Oh yes, Sir. I'm looking forward to it, Sir."

I pulled my cock out of my pants and said, “If you want a drink, boy, open your mouth!”

Wolf looked up at me for a second, and then, to my mild surprise, opened his mouth as wide as he could. I felt the rush of warmth as the piss began to flow from my dick, splashing on Wolf’s chest and neck until I adjusted my aim and directed the hot stream directly into his mouth. I could see his throat muscles working as he swallowed my piss as fast as he could. I kept the stream going into his mouth until I felt my bladder emptying, and then drew the stream of hot piss down Wolf’s body until I was pissing on his thickening cock. I shot the last few dribbles onto his crotch, saying “That was your only drink, slave. I hope you enjoyed it!”

His only reply was a soft moan. I looked down at my slave laying spread-eagled in the blazing sun, his muscled body now covered in a mixture of piss and sweat, totally helpless and totally at my mercy, and decided that I was the luckiest leather master in the world to have a slave like Wolf! He constantly was a source of pleasure and surprises to me. He normally didn’t like taking my piss, and I didn’t usually press him on the issue because I respected him and his limits, so he had surprised me by wanting me to piss on him and drinking my piss now.

I then leered at him “I think we need something else to help attract the ants, don’t you, boy?” Wolf just nodded his head silently.

“O.K. Then boy, maybe this will do it,” I said, pulling a small plastic squeeze bottle from my pocket.

I had borrowed it from the ranch’s dining room after explaining to Chuck what I wanted it for. He had thought it was a “Really neat and totally evil thing to do” to my slave, and said he would try to come out to the cabin in the afternoon to help me torture Wolf.

I held the bottle out over Wolf’s body and began to run a stream of honey down over his thick cock and balls. He moaned as the sweet liquid coated his dick, knowing it would bring every ant in yards in every direction to torment him. I ran a stream of honey up the middle of Wolf’s abs to his chest and coated both of his erect nipples. Then the streams ran down into his deep armpits and down onto the ground, giving the ants more places to torment my slave.

By the time I had walked to the cabin to put the honey container away and rinse off my hands in the sink and then walked back to Wolf, the ants were already starting to swarm onto his naked body. He moaned and squirmed in his bondage as he felt the crawling sensations on his skin.

The moaning grew louder as the ants spread across his skin; concentrating on his thick, erect cock and his hard tits. Soon, his dick, tits and armpits, and anywhere else the honey was on his skin, was covered with dozens of crawling, biting ants. The struggling and twisting of his muscled body was even more intense now, as he desperately tried to escape the torture of the ants that felt like they were literally eating him alive! At least, that's what he told me later.

I grinned evilly down at my desperately straining slave and said, "How are you doing now, boy? Is this what you wanted, to be used for ant food, boy?"

Wolf moaned, "Oh God, yes, Sir! I love it, Sir!"

I decided to increase the level of torture for Wolf to endure since he seemed to be enjoying himself so much. While walking back to the cabin, I noticed a shirtless figure on horseback approaching the clearing from the direction of the main ranch buildings. By the time I had picked up the next toys I was planning to use to torment Wolf, I could see that it was Chuck, the ranch owner. I waited until he rode up to me and then said, "Well, I'm glad to see that you made it. I was just about to start having some real fun with Wolf!"

Chuck grinned at me and said "Good, I'm glad I could get free for a bit. I've been looking forward to working on that muscle stud of yours ever since I first saw him. He's a hot guy! Of course, knowing you like I do, I wouldn't expect anything else!"

When Chuck dismounted from his horse, the first thing he did was give me a big hug. I felt a rush of pleasure at the feel of his hot bare chest pressed against mine, and immediately thought of another way to torment Wolf, with Chuck's help.

We walked over to where Wolf was staked out, and watched his futile struggles against the restraints holding him spread-eagled on the ground. The number of ants crawling on his muscled body seemed to have lessened somewhat, as the honey on his skin mixed with his sweat and ran down off his chest onto the ground. I could see that his nipples and his cock and balls were covered with lots of tiny red bite marks that would probably itch for days, so Wolf would really remember this session for a while!

Wolf looked up at us, standing over him and only moaned softly at the sight of the new torture devices I was carrying. I knelt down at Wolf's head, with one knee on either side of his head and ordered him, "Open your mouth as wide as you can, slave!"

He immediately did so, allowing me to slip a leather wrapped metal ring into his mouth. Positioned behind his teeth, it would keep Wolf from being able to close his mouth until the ring was removed. I then took the two long leather thongs on either side of the ring and, ordering Wolf to lift his head, tied them behind his head, securing the ring in place. Wolf groaned as I allowed him to put his head back down on the ground, knowing he would have to endure hours more torture at the hands of both Chuck and myself until I allowed the scene to end.

I looked up at Chuck, standing there watching me work on my slave and asked him with a wink, "Do you want to help me torture this Indian, cowboy?"

He sneered evilly at Wolf and said, "I sure do. Did you know that I had some ancestors that had been captured and tortured by Indians back in the pioneer days, and I've been waiting for a chance to repay them?"

I told him, "Well, here's your chance. He's stretched and helpless and he's yours to do whatever you want for a while!"

Wolf groaned loudly, not knowing that Chuck and I had set this whole scene up the previous day, while he was lounging around the pool. He groaned again when Chuck knelt down next to his body and began to run his fingertips over his stretched, sweaty torso. Chuck looked over at me and said, "What else to you have to use on this injun's body, that will really hurt? He looks like he needs to suffer some more!"

I told him, "Try these!" Wolf moaned through the ring when he saw what I was giving to Chuck to use on Wolf's body. It was the double row tit clamps with the biting teeth!

Wolf began to thrash and strain as Chuck worked the first clamp into position on his right tit. He let out an inarticulate howl of agony as the clamp was set on his already tender nipple, covered with ant bites. His sounds of agony increased when the other clamp was set in place on the other tit. Wolf's chest heaved and his muscles strained as he thrashed and twisted against his bonds, as the level of pain in his chest rose and peaked, until he adapted to the agony of the nipple clamps.

Chuck stood up and said, "Those look like they really hurt. Let's let him endure that for a while until we can see what else to do to this injun!"

I grinned at Chuck and said; "Well, he seems to like those so much, maybe you need to try these." And I handed him a handful of smaller, but still very painful biting metal clamps. Wolf began to scream again as Chuck knelt back down and began to put the clamps in place on the skin of Wolf's ball sack!

When he was done, I told him, "That works for me. I think he should wear those clamps for the rest of the day, don't you? Just think how much it's gonna hurt when we take them off!"

Chuck looked at me and said, "You know, that turned me on watching him suffer like that!"

I just smiled at him from where I was still kneeling at Wolf's head and told him, "Well then, come over here!"

Chuck stepped over Wolf's body until he was facing me, his crotch inches from my face. I reached up and ran my hands over Chuck's muscular body, feeling the warmth of his skin and the sweat trickling down his hard abs. Wolf moaned in a pleasurable agony as he realized what we were about to do. He loved to watch me have sex with another man, but he also suffered enormous frustration when he couldn't do anything but watch. I reached for Chuck's belt and undid it and then unfastened his jeans, allowing his erect eight-inch cock to pop out. Both Wolf and Chuck moaned when I leaned forward and ran my tongue up the length of the thick shaft. I then opened my mouth wider and sucked the thick head of Chuck's dick into my throat. He moaned again as he used his hands to hold my head in place while he began fucking my mouth. I reached up and started twisting his tits while he thrust his dick in and out of me. The sweat started flowing down his body as he worked harder and harder on my mouth. Wolf moaned helplessly as he was forced to watch me suck another man's cock only inches above his face without his being able to do a thing.

Finally, Chuck gasped; "God, I'm gonna cum, Eric!"

I pulled back from his cock and told him to shoot his load all over my helpless slave. He turned and pumped his dick until his load erupted from his cock, spraying over Wolf's gleaming torso. Wolf groaned as the hot sperm splashed on his body, and then, with an inarticulate yowl, he shot a no-hands load of his own. Very few things could force Wolf to shoot without jacking his cock, or having someone jack it for him, but I guess the combination of excruciating pain in his tits and balls from the clamps, the itching of the ant bites all over his body, the developing sunburn on his torso and legs, and being forced to watch me suck another man's cock just inches from his face was enough to do it!

Chuck was gasping for air as he caught his breath after his orgasm. "Damn, Eric, that injun slave of yours is really a horny one, isn't he? I've never seen anyone do that before! Shit!"

I grinned down at Wolf, the cum from two more loads splashed across his spread-eagled torso, winked at him, and said; "Yeah, he's pretty hot. Unfortunately, he didn't ask permission before cumming, so I guess I'll have to punish him even harder." Wolf only whimpered softly, the ring in his mouth keeping him from speaking.

As I stood up over Wolf, Chuck said to me; "I think I need to repay the favor, don't you?" as he knelt in front of me and worked my erect cock out of my jeans.

I groaned with pleasure as Chuck sucked my hot dick deeply into his mouth, while Wolf groaned in frustration as he realized he was going to have to watch another hot cocksucking session without being able to do anything. Even though he had shot a huge load just minutes before, Wolf's cock began to swell and thicken again as he watched Chuck deep-throat my shaft. I had been sucked off by Chuck many times before, and I knew he was an expert cocksucker.

Within five minutes or so, I growled; "Shit, I'm gonna cum!"

Chuck looked up into my eyes and said; "Give me your load, Eric. I want that hot cum in my mouth!"

He sucked my cock back into his mouth just as I threw my head back and howled as I shot a huge load down his throat. I yelled and groaned as the cum filled his mouth. Chuck swallowed as fast as he could, taking my load of sperm into his belly!

Wolf was only able to moan in frustration as he was forced to watch me shoot my load into Chuck's mouth.

Finally, I pulled my softening dick from Chuck's mouth and panted; "God damn, that mouth of yours is like a vacuum cleaner!"

Chuck leered at me as he stood up, licking the last of my load from his lips. "Well, it's not every day I get to suck off such a hot muscleman as you, Eric. You know you're the best-built guy I've ever had sex with! But who knows, maybe I'll get a chance to work on that hot muscle boy slave of yours before you guys leave!"

I winked at him and said loudly enough for Wolf to hear; "Well, come by the barn later tonight after dark, and maybe you can suck him off after I'm done torturing him. Just imagine what a hard flogging is gonna feel like on that sunburn! He's gonna welt up so nicely!" Wolf groaned and whimpered at my words, knowing that this day of torture was far from over!

Chuck and I went into the cabin to talk, leaving Wolf to endure more time staked out spread-eagled in the blazing sun with the clamps torturing his tits and balls. We went in to discuss the final scene I had planned for Wolf, to be done the night before we would leave to go home. I had decided it was time to give Wolf the permanent markings he had always wanted, and it was time to brand his nipples with the custom made irons I had had made weeks ago!

Chapter Eight
Agony

Chuck and I spent a couple of hours in the cabin talking and catching up with each other, as I hadn't seen much of him since he had bought the ranch from an uncle and moved out to the property about a year earlier to convert it from a working cattle ranch into the torture ranch it now was. We also talked about the specifics of what I would need to have arranged before I did Wolf's branding, such as arranging how to heat the irons to red-hot for branding Wolf's chest, arranging for first-aid supplies in my cabin and other plans for Wolf's next sessions of torture both in and out of the torture chamber, including the ultimate test of Wolf's physical strength, not just his ability to endure pain.

Finally, I noticed that it was getting late in the afternoon, and I asked Chuck if he wanted to help me torture Wolf one more time before I released him from his bondage for the day.

He grinned at me and told me; "Hell yes, I'll help you torture him! But first, there's something else I want to do!"

At that, he leaned towards me and, bending down, began to suck on my left nipple. I moaned softly at the feel of his mouth on my tit and his hands stroking my body. Chuck was an expert on working on my tits, as he had done it many times in the years we had known each other. After a few minutes of sucking and nibbling on my left tit, he slowly worked his way across my chest to my right nipple and started giving it the same treatment with his mouth. I let him continue for a few minutes then I lay back on the bed in the cabin and told Chuck to work on my pits. He leered at me, then buried his face in my right armpit. I groaned at the feel of his hot mouth sucking and licking out my pit. I knew Chuck was a sucker for hot, sweaty pits, and he would stay right there, with his face buried in my armpits for as long as I would let him. When he had licked out my right pit for a few minutes, he worked his way across my chest to my left armpit, which he then proceeded to lick out just as thoroughly. I knew that if he liked my armpits, he would go absolutely crazy for Wolf's hot, sweat filled pits, stretched out like they were in the blazing hot sun.

Finally, reluctantly, I slowly pushed him off of my chest, where he was laying.

"We really need to get back out there and finish torturing Wolf!" I told him.

Chuck just smirked at me and said; "Don't worry, I'll probably get to finish before the two of you leave."

I just gave him a look and said; "Sure of yourself, aren't you?"

He answered; "Hell, yes, I've known you way too long, Eric!"

"Bitch!"

"And damn proud of it, too!"

At that, we both broke up. Chuck was right. He probably would get to finish his tit sucking, pit eating, and anything else that popped up before Wolf and I left the ranch. When we had calmed down, we walked out to where Wolf was lying spread-eagled in the blazing sun.

By now, the breath was rasping in his parched throat, since he wasn't able to close his mouth because of the ring gag I had inserted hours earlier. Wolf just lay there staked out in the sun, baking in the heat, his eyes closed and his brown torso glistening with sweat, highlighted by the silver of the metal clamps biting into his tits and ballsack, enduring one of the longest sessions of continuous torture I had ever subjected him to. He had been in bondage for longer periods of time, but had never been forced to endure that high of a level of pain, or so many different forms of pain, for so long.

When we walked up to him Wolf didn't open his eyes. I gave him a not-so-gentle nudge in the ribs with the toe of my boot. His eyes flew open wide as he gasped with pain and surprise at my kick.

I imagine the first things that he saw were two muscular, bare-chested men in denims and western boots, staring down at him from under cowboy hats.

"What do you think, Chuck, does he need more torture?" I growled, all business now.

"Yep, he needs to suffer more!" Chuck drawled.

"Is there anything you want to do to him before we really start to hurt this injun?" I asked Chuck, knowing what he wanted.

He grinned lustfully at me and said, "You bet there is. I've been waiting to do this ever since I first saw this stud boy of yours."

Dropping to his knees over Wolf's spread torso, Chuck lowered his face and began to eat out Wolf's sweat filled pits. Wolf groaned around the ring in his mouth as Chuck licked and bit the tender skin of Wolf's deep, sunburned armpits. Chuck's head bobbed up and down as he tortured my slave's torso by biting and stretching the skin of his tender pits with his teeth, then pulled on the hair in Wolf's pits with his fingers, drawing another loud groan from my slave.

I watched the torture for a few minutes, admiring the rippling muscles under the gleaming skin of Chuck's back, as well as enjoying the view of my own slave's magnificent physique enduring the torture.

Finally, I told Chuck it was time for the both of us to work on Wolf!

"I want you to kneel down and put one knee on either side of his head to keep him from moving too much. It's time to see just how much pain this Injun can take before he either passes out or cums!"

Wolf moaned loudly at that, and also from the expression on my face. He knew from experience that I meant business now. He also knew that I wouldn't injure him, but he wouldn't get any mercy, either. He closed his eyes briefly while he mentally prepared himself to endure the extreme torture that he was about to be subjected to.

Chuck dropped to his knees and pinned Wolf's head tightly between them. He was also kneeling on Wolf's hair, spread around his head, further immobilizing him.

I stepped between Wolf's wide spread legs and stared impassively down at my helpless slave. All Wolf could do was look back up at me. I saw a brief expression of anxiety on his face, which was then quickly replaced with one of anticipation.

I looked deeply into his brown eyes and asked Wolf; "Are you ready for some of the worst pain you've ever endured in your life, slave?"

He looked back up at me with an expression of total trust on his face, and gave me as much of a nod as he could with his head trapped between Chuck's knees. I gave him a nod, and a brief smile, and saw the smile in his eyes, even if he couldn't actually smile because of the ring in his mouth.

I looked at Chuck and asked him; "Do you still have your work gloves with you?"

He nodded; "Yep, still got 'em."

"O.K. Put 'em on and get ahold of those tit clamps. When I tell you to, take those clamps off his tits, grab those nipples and torture them hard! Harder than you've ever worked on anyone's nipples! I want to hear this Injun screaming in pain!"

Wolf whimpered loudly at the thought of the incredible pain he would be soon enduring. Even in the face of overwhelming torture, however, his cock began swelling and stiffening. Soon his dick was fully erect, arcing up over his washboard stomach muscles.

I lifted my right foot and slowly planted it on Wolf's swollen ball sack. He began to thrash and moan as I slowly began to increase the pressure on his tender nuts, digging the clamps deeper into the skin. His chest expanded to it's fullest as he moaned and then howled as I began to grind his balls into the dirt with my boot.

Chuck had his hands on Wolf's tit clamps, awaiting my order to open them. Until then, though, he was pulling and squeezing on the clamps, causing the teeth to dig deeper into Wolf's already tender nipples as his tits were stretched away from his thick pecs. Wolf's howls turned into screams of pain at the building agony in his balls and chest. He then screamed louder when I told Chuck; "All right, take those clamps off him and twist those tits as hard as you can!"

Wolf's screams became full-throated shrieks of raw agony when Chuck squeezed the clamps open and, removing them, began to twist and pull Wolf's raw, incredibly sensitive tits. The rough cowhide of Chuck's work gloves only increased the agony of Wolf's tit torture, while I pushed harder and harder on his balls with my boot, seemingly trying to flatten his nuts against the sun-baked ground.

My view of my tortured slave boy was one of the hottest things I had ever seen. Wolf's cock was swollen and purple under my boot, the veins throbbing and pulsating on the bloated, rock hard shaft. Every ripped and shredded muscle in his spread-eagled body was flexed and straining at its limit. The cords and veins stood out on Wolf's muscles and on his neck as he desperately tried to escape the agony ripping through his body. The sweat was flowing down the sides of his heaving ribcage and pooling in his deep armpits as his breath was coming in shorter and shorter gasps between the screams being ripped from his throat. I could actually see the rapid beating of Wolf's heart under the glistening skin of his chest. Chuck was pulling and twisting on Wolf's tits so hard that they were stretched a good two or three inches from his pumped pectoral muscles, and twisted almost completely around by Chuck's fingers. Chuck's biceps bulged with the strain of pulling on Wolf's tortured nipples as hard as he could from his kneeling position. Wolf's nipples were almost black from having had the biting nipple torture clamps digging into them for over four hours. His thick biceps and forearms were knotted with the effort to tear his hands loose from the ropes holding him helpless to the posts sunken securely into the ground, while the veins and muscles in his massive thighs bulged and strained as he twisted and struggled to free himself. The pain tearing throughout Wolf's body must have been absolutely incredible! Even I wasn't sure how much longer he could endure the torture he was being subjected to, and I knew that Wolf was a true masochist!

Wolf's screams of pain were growing louder and louder, even as Chuck was pulling and twisting his nipples as hard as he could, and I was grinding my boot into his crushed nuts.

I gritted my teeth and slowly increased the pressure on Wolf's nuts until I was literally standing with almost all my weight on his balls!

Chuck threw his head back and with a howl of effort, twisted and stretched Wolf's tits another inch or so from his straining pectorals. The sweat was running down Chuck's back and chest from the strain of torturing Wolf's nipples.

Finally, with one last ear-splitting shriek of total agony, Wolf's cock erupted with one of the biggest loads of cum I had ever seen my slave shoot! He was shrieking totally hysterically as the cum kept shooting from his cock, coating his heaving washboard abs and shooting across his pecs, even as I was yelling at Chuck to; "Yank on those tits harder! Rip 'em off that Injun's chest! Make him suffer like never before!"

Wolf gave one last raw scream as the cum finally finished shooting from his swollen cock. His eyes rolled back in his head as he slumped back on the ground, totally limp. At that, I asked Chuck to move out of the way so I could check on my slave.

As I checked to see that Wolf was all right and hadn't swallowed his tongue, Chuck asked if there was anything he could do to help. I thought for a moment and said; "Yeah, I seem to remember seeing a five gallon bucket next to the cabin. Would you mind going down to the river and filling it up for me?"

He stopped and said; "You know, that water comes down from melting snow in the mountains. It never gets very warm."

I looked up at him and said; "Good, I was counting on that!" I then went to work on my semi-coherent slave, who was still coming down from an incredible endorphin rush.

I lifted his head up and braced it on one of my knees, allowing me to reach under Wolf's head to untie the thongs holding the ring gag in his mouth. I carefully lowered his head back down and then worked the ring out of his mouth, gently massaging the sides of Wolf's face along his long, angular jaw line to prevent muscle spasms, as he was now able to close his mouth for the first time in several hours. I gently removed the clamps from his tortured ball sack, causing him to gasp and moan as each clamp was removed and I gently rubbed the skin to restore the circulation.

I leaned over Wolf's body and began to very gently suck on his nipples, enjoying the taste of his sweat mixed with the cum that had shot up onto his pecs during his explosive orgasm. He groaned at the feel of my mouth on his incredibly sensitive tits.

I worked on Wolf, comforting him and talking softly to him until Chuck walked back, carrying not one, but two buckets of icy river water. He grinned at me as he said; "I figured out what you wanted them for, and I figured you might need two!"

Wolf moaned up at me as I stood over his spread-eagled body and picked up one of the buckets. His moans turned into shrieks as I slowly started pouring the shockingly cold water over his over heated, sunburned, tortured body. Wolf struggled against his restraints as the cold water cascaded down on him. I knew one thing Wolf really hated was cold water. He didn't like swimming if the water was below eighty degrees, and this water couldn't have been over fifty at the very best.

He gasped and moaned as I finished emptying the first bucket on him and then moaned even louder as I picked up the second bucket.

"What's the matter, boy?" I taunted him. "You don't like this? I thought you would enjoy a cool, refreshing shower by now, boy! Besides, you stink! You smell like a high school locker room in July, boy!"

Chuck laughed at the analogy and Wolf even managed a smile just before I started slowly pouring the water on his helpless body again. He began to strain against the ropes holding him stretched out as the cold water poured down over him.

"Stop fighting it, boy, or I'll go and get more!" I told Wolf.

Using all his self-control, he relaxed and lay back flat on the ground as I finished his water torture.

Finally, I finished emptying the bucket on my shivering, battered slave boy. Sitting the bucket down, I knelt down next to Wolf and asked him; "How are you doing, boy? Are you all right now?"

He looked up at me and said; "Oh God, Sir, That was wonderful, Sir! Thank you, thank you, and thank you, Sir! I've waited for such a long time to be staked out all day, Sir! It was just … it was …"

At that, Wolf's eyes rolled back into his head again, and he just started to mutter to himself in something that sounded like a mixture of Spanish and Apache.

Startled, Chuck looked down and said; "Goddamn, is he all right, Eric?"

I told him; "I've seen this before. He's just over stimulated. It's not a really big deal, but I think we need to untie him now."

Chuck and I spent the next few minutes untying the ropes holding Wolf to the stakes. I slowly moved his legs together and slowly moved his arms down to his sides. I knelt next to Wolf stroking his face until his bloodshot eyes focused, and he smiled weakly up at me.

"Welcome back, boy. You were really gone for a few minutes there! Do you feel like trying to sit up now, boy?"

Wolf nodded and slowly pushed himself up to a sitting position. I held his shoulders as he swayed a bit before his head cleared. He then slowly worked himself up to his knees, and finally got up on his feet. He staggered a bit before I wrapped my arms around his shoulders for support.

"I am so proud of you, boy!" I softly told him. "I've never seen anyone take torture like that before! I love you so much!"

Wolf looked up into my eyes and told me; "I love you, too Sir! That was unbelievable, Sir. I can't describe how it felt. Just lying there for hours in the sun, helpless, at your mercy, Sir. The ants, and the clamps on me. And then being tortured by both of you. It was unreal, Sir. It was one of my deepest and oldest fantasies finally coming true. I've wanted that done to me ever since I was about ten years old, Sir!"

I could tell by the way Wolf was babbling on that he was still a bit out of it, so I told him we were going to go inside the cabin so he could recover. He just nodded as I helped him walk across the clearing and into the welcome coolness of the cabin. Once inside I got Wolf a bottle of water from the fridge, but told him to drink it slowly, to prevent any stomach cramps.

Chuck accompanied us inside and asked me; "Is there anything you need, Eric?"

I said; "Yeah, I think we're gonna need a ride back to the ranch, because I really don't think Wolf has another mile walk left in him right now!"

Chuck smiled at Wolf and said; "I wouldn't think he has anything left after today. I've seen some heavy scenes since I bought this place, but nothing like what he's taken today. That is one hell of a slave you've got there, Eric!"

I smiled at Wolf as well while we sat on the bed, my arms wrapped tightly around his body, holding him tightly to my chest. "Yeah, he's all right. I think I'll keep him for a while longer!"

Chuck laughed and said; "Hell, I don't blame you there. I'll go and get the jeep and drive you both back. Don't worry about your stuff, it'll be safe here until I can get one of my boys to come out and collect it for you and take the horse back to the barn. You just take care of that hot boy of yours. He's a real find."

After Chuck left, I turned all my attention to Wolf. He was sitting on the bed with his eyes closed, his head resting on my chest. I stroked his long hair, still wet with the river water and matted with dirt and mud, without saying anything, just holding him tightly. After a few minutes, I felt his body begin to shake as the emotions worked up to the surface, and Wolf began to cry in my arms. I let him empty out his feelings in a flood of tears that lasted for a good five minutes.

Finally, I felt him calming down and looked down into his bloodshot eyes. He smiled wanly at me and said; "God, now I know what a hot dog feels like on a grill, Sir."

I laughed at the incongruity of his statement, telling him; "Well, you always did have nice buns, boy. 'Hot Dog-Buns. That's a joke, son!'" I said in my best Foghorn Leghorn voice.

Wolf looked at me for a moment like I had lost my mind, then broke up laughing. I knew he was going to be fine. If I could make Wolf laugh after a hard scene, everything was going to be O.K.

We sat in the cabin, talking and laughing until I heard the sound of a vehicle approaching. In a moment Chuck stuck his head in the door and asked; "Everything all right, Eric? Is Wolf O.K.?"

I told him; "Oh yeah, I think he's gonna survive." I looked into Wolf's eyes and seeing the mischief there, asked him; "You do plan on surviving, don't you boy? I'd hate to have to plan on finding a replacement for you! You have my permission to answer in front of Chuck."

Wolf sighed dramatically and said; "Well, if you insist, Sir, I guess I'll just have to hang on at least another day. I wouldn't want you to have to go to all that trouble!"

We all started laughing at his obvious theatrics, and then Chuck said; "God, Eric, If he can find something to laugh about after a day like his, I guess Wolf really is something special!"

Chuck had finally figured out something I'd known since the first day I met Wolf!

I asked Wolf if there was anything else he wanted to do before we went back to the main ranch area. He smiled and said, "With your permission, Sir, I'd like to thank Chuck for helping you to torture me today. It hurt so good, Sir!"

I smiled back and told him, "Go ahead, boy!"

Wolf dropped to his knees in front of Chuck and, reaching out, unzipped his jeans. Chuck closed his eyes and groaned when Wolf sucked his thickening cock deeply into his mouth and then began to slowly pump it deeper and deeper into his throat.

Wolf's expert cocksucking lasted for just a few minutes before Chuck moaned, "I'm gonna shoot. Oh God, I'm gonna cum!" At that, Wolf pulled Chuck's throbbing cock out of his mouth and began to jack it furiously. With a loud moan, Chuck shot several long, thick streams of creamy cum across Wolf's sweat glazed chest. Wolf continued to pump Chuck's dick, until the last of the sperm had been milked from my friend's cock. Wolf then stood up between us; Chuck's cum running down over his thick chest, until Chuck unexpectedly bent over and began to lick his own cum from Wolf's massive pecs!

Chuck continued his licking until all of his own sperm had been cleaned off Wolf's chest, along with a lot of the sweat. Wolf moaned at the feel of Chuck's hot tongue lightly licking his tender, tortured nipples. Chuck then cleaned out my boy's deep armpits once more with his tongue, much more gently this time.

We rode back to the main ranch buildings with Chuck in his jeep, and I slowly walked my sun burned, battered, dirt and mud encrusted and totally exhausted slave boy across the yard to our cabin. I noticed that we attracted a lot of attention from the other guys that saw us. I had the feeling that we would be a major topic of gossip and speculation at dinner that night.

I told Wolf to wait in the cabin and relax while I got us both something to eat from the dining room, as he hadn't eaten a thing all day. We both agreed that Wolf was too tired to try to go to the dining room for dinner, much less to the barn for more torture that night, contrary to what I had told Chuck a few hours earlier in the day Even Wolf had his limits, and I think we had just about reached them with today's session of torture.

I had originally planned on testing my slave to the outer limits of his strength and endurance, but I didn't want to go so far that I ended up injuring my slave.

As I picked up a couple of meals to go, I had time to reflect on the events of the last couple of days. I was really proud of what Wolf had endured, and felt that he had earned a day off before I subjected him to his ultimate test of strength and endurance. I decided not to tell him what I had planned for his final torture, since I was hoping that Wolf could rise to whatever challenge I presented him with. If he passed my final test, I would know that Wolf was the perfect slave, and my long quest to find the one man to spend the rest of my life with would finally be over!

Chapter Nine
Endurance

After I had returned from the dining room with a couple of meals to go for Wolf and myself, and we had eaten, I stripped off my clothes and told Wolf to go into the bathroom of the cabin. He got up and did so, but he was sagging with weariness. I knew that I had pushed him right to the edge of his endurance, and that was why I decided to give him a day off before his next, and final, test of strength and stamina before I gave him his ultimate reward, his brandings.

We went into the bathroom and I turned on the shower. Wolf moaned softly as he stepped into the spray of warm water.

"Lean up against the wall, boy." I told him. Wolf braced himself on the wall of the shower as I started to gently wash his broad back with the liquid soap I liked to use. I heard him moaning and groaning softly as I worked his muscles with my fingers.

I reached out and, pushing his hair forward, began to massage his thick shoulders, digging into his rock-hard traps and delts. After a few minutes, I felt his muscles begin to relax as the combination of my massage, and the warm water began to work.

Wolf groaned; "Oh yeah! God, that feels good, Sir! Please, don't stop!"

I continued my massage of his thick, hard-muscled back, slowly working my way all the way down to his firm, rounded ass, and then down the thick columns of his legs. By the time I had finished his legs, Wolf was leaning against the shower wall, softly moaning continually with pleasure. I told him to turn around, and I started back up the front of his legs, gently cleaning his sun burned shins and thighs.

Wolf gasped and groaned with pleasure when I started to gently stroke his cock and balls, causing his dick to start to stiffen and swell. He moaned louder when I leaned in and took the head of his cock into my mouth and began to work it with my tongue.

I knelt in front of my slave-boy lover in the shower, with the warm water cascading down over our bodies, sucking his thick cock, until he took hold of my head and, holding it still, began to fuck my mouth. Wolf thrust his dick deeper and deeper into my willing mouth until, with a loud groan, he shot a load of his hot, salty, and bittersweet cum deeply into my throat.

He panted; "Oh yeah, take it, Sir, please take it!" as he filled my mouth with his load. I slowly swallowed his sperm, thoroughly enjoying the taste.

Finally, Wolf let go of my head, and I stood up in front of him and wrapped my arms around his hard muscled body, and held him while was panting and gasping from his orgasm. We stood there for a few minutes, as the water washed down over us, just enjoying the intimate feel of our bond of closeness. I knew for sure that I had never felt such a deep love for any other man in my life.

Finally, I released him, saying; "Thank you, boy."

Wolf looked at me and said quizzically "Thank you for what, Sir?"

I smiled at him and said; "Just for being you, boy. The love of my life!"

He leaned towards me, kissed me deeply and whispered; "Thank you for being the master I've desired all my life, Sir!"

I then finished my washing of Wolf's hard torso, working my way across his washboard abs, over his ribcage and up to his thick, sculpted pecs. I gently rinsed his raw, tender nipples, causing Wolf to groan softly. I then told him to lean back and put his hands behind his head, giving me access to his deep armpits, and his baseball sized biceps.

When I was done with his body, I spent a few minutes washing and then conditioning his magnificent mane of thick, black hair. I loved Wolf's hair, to be honest, and didn't mind the effort it took to keep it thick and shiny. I hugged him and said; "Let's get out of this water before I turn into a prune, boy."

Wolf chuckled at that, we dried off and I brushed out his hair. Finally, I told Wolf that I thought that it was time for him to go to bed, as it had been a long day for both of us, but especially for him.

Before I put him to bed, however, I got out a tube of a cream that Chuck had recommended for bug bites to help control itching and soreness, and coated Wolf's cock and balls, and tits with it. I then put him in his own bed and asked him; "How's that, boy? Do you think you'll be able to not scratch, or do I need to tie your hands to the bedposts tonight?"

Wolf sleepily told me that he would be fine, and I guess that he was, as he fell asleep within minutes of his head hitting the pillow, even though it was just a bit past sunset.

The next day, we both took it easy and enjoyed some of the amenities that the ranch had to offer, such as horseback riding, hanging out by the pool and doing a light workout in the small, but nicely equipped weightlifting gym in one of the outbuildings of the ranch. In the afternoon, though, I informed Wolf that he had another test of endurance coming up the next day. I didn't tell him what I had planned, but rather told him to be ready for anything. I could tell by his expression that he was both apprehensive, and excited at the thought of more torture.

We went to the barn that night for more play in the dungeon, and while there, Chuck finally got his chance to suck off Wolf while I used my riding crop to torture Wolf's still sunburned torso. I spread-eagled Wolf on a St. Andrew's cross and worked his chest with the crop and floggers, until he pumped a thick load of sperm into Chuck's mouth. Then, just for the fun of it, I moved Wolf over to where I had had him spread-eagled our first night, between the beams, and announced to all the guys there that anyone who wanted to play with my slave's spread body could do so, as long as there wasn't any penetration without my express permission.

I enjoyed watching Wolf moaning and writhing in his chains while two hot, young blonde surfer type boys, who were twin brothers and slaves of a tall, well-built African-American master, sucked and chewed on his tits and ate out his armpits. While the twins tortured Wolf's nipples, another boy was sucking on his cock and chewing on his nuts, while Donald's boy Jay, had his face buried between the globes of Wolf's hot ass. Wolf groaned and struggled in his bondage, his body dripping sweat, moaning at the feel of four hot mouths working on his helpless body at the same time, until the boy sucking his dick managed to coax another load of sperm out of Wolf's now tender, sore cock. Wolf slumped down, only held up by the restraints on his wrists. I left him there, helpless and exhausted, and forced him to watch as the twin slaves went to work on my body, sucking on my nipples and playing with my tit rings, licking my sweaty pecs and abs, and eating out my armpits while Jay sucked my cock until I blew a thick load of cum into his hot, sucking mouth. Donald was watching, and as soon as Jay had swallowed my load, Donald stuffed his hard eight inch dick down his boy's throat and fucked his mouth until he came as well. The fourth boy had gone to work on the huge, ten inch ebony shaft of the other master and sucked him to an explosive orgasm.

Finally, after about three hours in the barn, I decided that we had both had enough for the night, as I had already cum twice, and Wolf looked to be on the brink of tears whenever someone went to work on his now incredibly sensitive tits. I had counted at least fifteen different guys working on Wolf's nipples and armpits, or his cock and balls, or just feeling and admiring his helpless, muscled body while he was stretched in his chains and I had had at least as many hot men worshipping my body, licking my boots, or otherwise servicing me.

On the way back to our cabin, I reminded Chuck of what I would need him to arrange for Wolf's next torture session. He smiled lustfully and said; "It's all set. I'll see you guys tomorrow in the corral about eleven."

The next morning, at breakfast in the dining room, while Wolf was still keeling on the floor next to the table, I announced to the guys there that if Wolf could pass his next test, he would be allowed the privileges of being able to speak without permission, and that he could use the furniture.

One of the guys there asked; "What are you gonna do to him, Sir?"

I just grinned evilly down at Wolf, and said; "Come to the corral at eleven and see!"

I heard Wolf moan softly at that. I gave him a nudge with my foot. He looked up into my eyes, and I gave him a wink. He smiled back up at me, and then turned his eyes back to the floor, as a proper slave should do.

When it came near time for us to go to the corral, I told Wolf to change into a pair of denims and his combat boots, but no shirt, and ponytail his hair. Both of us then walked bare-chested from our cabin to the corral, where there were at least thirty guys waiting. Wolf still didn't have any idea of what I was going to do to him, until we walked into the corral, and there was Chuck and Jimmy, his top hand and lover, waiting with two of the cow ponies the ranch hands used for herding the small herd of cows on the property. I led Wolf to the center of the corral between the horses.

He moaned softly, so only I could hear; "You have got to be kidding, Sir!"

I grabbed his ponytail and yanked it tight, snapping his head back, snarling in his face; "Do I look like I'm kidding, boy? DO I?"

Taken aback, Wolf stammered; "No … No, Sir, I'm sorry, Sir. Please forgive me, Sir!"

I softened my expression and told him; "That's better, boy! Now get ready!"

Wolf stood silently, breathing deeply, loading his lungs with as much oxygen as he could, his thick chest rising and falling, while Chuck tied ropes from the harnesses on the horses to heavy leather restraints that I had buckled on Wolf's wrists. When the ropes were attached, Chuck and Jimmy mounted their horses and slowly walked them apart, until the ropes drew Wolf's arms out tight from his sides.

I told the crowd of guys watching that if Wolf could endure fifteen minutes of the torture from the horses, that I would give him the privilege of using the furniture and being able to speak without my specific permission each time.

I asked Wolf; "Ready, boy?"

He swallowed deeply and then nodded silently. I looked at Chuck and told him to go ahead and try to tear my slave apart.

He and Jimmy spurred their horses, in a seeming effort to tear Wolf's arms out of joint. Wolf threw back his head and howled, as every muscle in his sculpted torso stood out in sharp relief at the incredible strain he had to suddenly endure. Unbelievably, his body was able to withstand the awesome pull of the horses. His shoulder and back muscles knotted and quivered with the effort required just to keep his arm joints together. His broad, flaring lats seemed to widen and knot in a thick bunching of rock-hard muscle, creating even more of a V-taper from Wolf's incredible shoulders down to his narrow waist.

Within seconds, the sweat started to flow down his brown skin from his deep, straining armpits, and down across his broad, writhing back muscles and heaving, bulging pecs.

Wolf stood like a statue, his arms stretched out to the sides, while his chest heaved and his ab muscles flexed with every breath. Every rib in his thick ribcage stood out in sharp relief under his gleaming skin. It actually looked to me like Wolf's shoulders were being stretched several inches wider then they usually were. His eyes were closed and his handsome face was contorted in a grimace of total agony, his teeth gritted and his jaw clenched as his strength was tested to the very edge of his endurance.

I knew that if Wolf was really hurting, or if he felt himself being injured, he would scream out our safe word, and I would immediately stop the torture. I also knew how strong Wolf really was and had told Chuck how hard to have the horses pull on his arms. Chuck assured me that the horses were superbly trained.

I heard comments like; "*Oh My God*!" and "*I don't believe it!*" and "*There's no way in Hell he can take that for fifteen minutes!!*" from some of the guys watching.

Wolf stood helpless while the horses strained at the ropes, the sweat flowing down his torso and staining the top of his denims. The veins bulged on his biceps and down his forearms and across his pecs. The breath rasped in and out between his clenched teeth while he struggled to endure the single hardest test of strength he had ever suffered. His ponytail was soaked with sweat and stuck to his knotted back. I looked at my watch and called out to the crowd; "Two minutes!" Then I stepped into the center of the corral, behind Wolf's straining body, and wrapped my arms around his torso. I marveled at the feel of his incredibly hard back and shoulder muscles, straining to their limits, against my bare chest. I heard Wolf groaning and grunting with the effort he was putting into enduring the torture I was subjecting him to.

I whispered into his ear; "Do you think you can take it for the full time, boy?"

He grunted; "I'll try, Sir!"

I then stepped in front of him and stroked my hands up and down his straining chest and ab muscles, loving the look and the feel of the sweaty skin rippling over every muscle and rib. The striations in the muscles of Wolf's chest and abs were clearly visible under his gleaming skin. I stepped back from my straining slave and loudly announced; "Five minutes!"

Next to add to his torture, I waved the twin slave boys in from the crowd and told them to torture Wolf's nipples with their mouths and teeth while he was helpless to do anything about it. I had arranged with their master for them to be able to help with Wolf's torture. They bent down and began to suck and chew on his sweaty pecs and nipples, causing Wolf to moan loudly at the additional torment, as he was unable to do anything about the two hot mouths working on his body.

I allowed the twins to torture Wolf's chest for just a few minutes before I told them that it was enough for now, but that they would be able to worship my pecs and tits later as a reward for their help. I looked at my watch and announced; "Ten minutes!"

To my surprise, some of the guys in the crowd watching Wolf's struggle started to softly chant; "Wolf, Wolf, Wolf!" then others joined in, until the whole corral echoed with the cry of; "WOLF! -WOLF! -WOLF!"

Amazingly, Wolf seemed to draw strength from the chanting. He opened his eyes, and I saw they were blazing with a ferocity I had rarely seen from him before. Then, to my utter astonishment, he threw his head back and with an ear-splitting, almost inhuman howl, began to bend his arms in at the elbows, his biceps flexed to the absolute max! The veins popped out on his amazing body from neck to abs, as the horses stretching him actually started to have to back up.

The chanting died away as the crowd went absolutely silent at this display of almost impossible strength, until one of the guys in the crowd watching Wolf's ultimate test of strength hollered; *"THERE'S NO FUCKING WAY!! HE CAN'T ACTUALLY BE DOING THAT!!"*

He managed to keep bending his arms until, unbelievably, Wolf managed to pull his hands in until his elbows were bent like he was doing a bicep pose in a bodybuilding contest, the muscles of his arms and chest quivering and shaking with the effort. His huge biceps looked like they were going to explode at any second!

The sweat was pouring down his torso like someone had just emptied a bucket of water over his body. Wolf managed to hold this impossibly difficult position, howling continuously at the top of his lungs, until I hollered "Fifteen minutes!" Then I told Chuck; "O.K. I think that's enough."

He and Jimmy reined back on their horses, and as the ropes started to slacken, Wolf sagged to his knees in the dust of the corral. He started to moan loudly as the pressure on his arms slowly eased. I stepped back up in front of him and knelt down so we were face-to-face in the corral. I untied the ropes from the thick leather restraints on Wolf's wrists.

"Don't drop your arms, boy," I instructed him. "Keep them out to the side!"

Wolf nodded to me, too totally exhausted to speak, but I knew that he knew what I wanted him to do to prevent any injury. He moaned again as I grasped his left arm and, feeling the still quivering muscles, slowly lowered it down to his side. He gasped at the pain in his joints, but accepted it as a consequence of his torture. I repeated the lowering of his other arm, and then began to rub and massage his shoulders. All at once, we were surrounded by most of the men who had witnessed Wolf's test of strength. They started to applaud and cheer when I wrapped my arms around my totally exhausted slave and kissed him deeply. Wolf only had the strength left to hold on to me as he leaned his head against my chest and started to weep as a result of the torture he had successfully endured in front of everyone at the ranch.

We knelt there in the dirt for a good ten minutes before I asked Wolf; "Do you have the strength to stand up, boy?"

Wolf nodded and said; "I'll try, Sir.

We slowly got up to another round of applause, and then we were escorted to the edge of the corral to some seats by a group of the guys.

Chuck came up with a couple of bottles of cold water for us, which we gratefully accepted. Wolf and I just sat while he recovered some of his strength. We accepted the congratulations and compliments from the guys who had witnessed Wolf's incredible feat of strength. I told Wolf to stand up, and I loudly called for the attention of the guys left surrounding us.

When they were quiet, I reached out and unbuckled Wolf's thick leather slave collar from around his throat and replaced it with a much thinner one that I had put in my pocket before leaving our cabin.

I announced to the crowd and to Wolf; "This signifies the granting of your privileges, boy. You are still my slave, but as of right now, while at the ranch, you have earned my permission to use the furniture, and to speak freely. Congratulations, boy!" Applause broke out from the guys still around us.

Finally, I told Wolf it was time to go back to the cabin and clean off the sweat that was still flowing off his body. I didn't tell him that I intended to clean it off with my tongue, but he discovered that when we got back to the cabin. I tied him in a standing spread-eagled position, echoing the position he was in while the horses were trying to tear his arms out of joint. Chuck had equipped the cabins with eye hooks screwed into various places in the wooden beams and framing of the cabin, so it was easy to bind Wolf in the exact position I wanted him in.

I stripped off my clothes, stepped up to him, wrapped my arms around his still sweaty torso and kissed him deeply. When I finally broke the kiss, I murmured in his ear; "Here's another reward for being the strongest, bravest and most incredible slave I've ever seen, boy!"

Wolf closed his eyes and moaned softly when I started to slowly and teasingly give his entire torso a tongue bath. I started by chewing gently on his left ear lobe, and then stuck my tongue deeply in his ear. I worked my way down his long jaw line and back up the other side of his face to his other ear. Wolf moaned almost constantly for the next half hour while I worshipped his spread body from ears to navel, working on his thick nipples for a good five minutes each. I went down his back just as slowly, making love to every ripple and bulge of muscle with my mouth and my tongue, licking up the streams of sweat that were still flowing down his rock hard muscles. I breathed deeply with my face buried in Wolf's thick, luxurious mane of hair, loving his man scent. I ran my tongue over the veins on his thick biceps and triceps, licked out his deep, sweaty armpits and finally knelt in front of my moaning, sweating, incredibly aroused slave.

Wolf gasped; "Oh shit, yes, Sir, God yes!" when I started to chew and mouth his thick, rock-hard cock through the fabric of his denims. He groaned and growled even louder as I slowly teased his denims open, using my teeth to pull the zipper down.

Finally, I just couldn't wait any longer, and sucked Wolf's thick, throbbing cock all the way into my mouth. Wolf groaned and struggled against his bonds as I sucked his cock and twisted his nipples until finally, he threw his head back and, with a howl of lust, filled my mouth with a huge load of hot, salty cum.

I kept sucking, teasing, and chewing on his cock until Wolf gasped; "Please, Sir, please stop! Oh God, please stop! I can't take any more, Sir!" I knew his cock got very sensitive just after an orgasm, and I often tortured him this way.

I grinned up at him, past his heaving, sweat-streaked chest, and said; "Remember what I said the other day about paybacks, boy!"

He gasped; "Yes, Sir. You're right, Sir!"

I stood up and wrapped my arms around his helpless torso and giving him an evil smile, said; "Of course I'm right, boy. I'm the Master. Masters are always right!"

Wolf started to chuckle and then said; "Except when they're wrong, that is!"

I looked at him in mock horror! "A master that's wrong? Perish the thought!"

We both broke up at that. I was laughing so hard it was difficult to untie Wolf, and he was giggling almost hysterically. Endorphins again, I guess.

Finally we both calmed down, then I told Wolf to strip. I gathered him into my arms and flopped back on the bed, with him lying on top of me.

"Seriously, boy I want to tell you how incredibly proud I am of you! I wasn't sure anyone could take the tortures you have endured the last few days. You are one in a million, boy!"

Wolf smiled down at me and said; "Well, I have to do it, Sir. I have the greatest Master in the world!" and then just bent his head down and started to lick my chest between my pecs. His worship of my muscled physique continued for quite a while, with Wolf running his tongue over almost every square inch on my body.

Finally, he whispered into my ear; "Please, Sir, fuck me! Fuck me hard and deep, Sir!"

No other words were needed. The only sounds we made for the next hour or so were the sounds of two men who loved each other deeply making passionate love.

When we were done, and were both lying wrapped in each others arms, dripping with sweat, I told him; "I love you, boy, and I'm going to have something for you. But, you'll have to wait for it. It's a surprise. Actually, I have two!"

Wolf smiled back and said; "You know I always love your surprises, Sir!"

What Wolf didn't know, however, was that one of his surprises was going to be permanent!

Chapter Ten

Branded

Over the next couple of days, while Wolf was recovering from the almost unimaginable tortures I had submitted him to, I secretly finalized my plans to give him the reward he had so completely earned, his brandings. I also had another surprise for him as well.

As we relaxed by the pool or anywhere else on the ranch, we had a constant stream of compliments and congratulations from the other guys who had witnessed our activities of the last few days, both in the torture barn, and outside in the corral. Wolf was lucky in that being naturally dark-skinned, he didn't peel from the sunburn he suffered from his stake-out, but just turned an even darker shade of coppery bronze. I jokingly suggested to him that I might have to stake him out again, only face down this time to even out his tan. Wolf just grinned and said; "Whenever you're ready, Sir!"

However, I did notice to my amusement, that whenever we lay out by the pool, Wolf spent most of his time lying on his stomach, letting his back and butt get a dose of sun. I enjoyed our time by the pool, however, since I enjoyed being able to rub sun tan oil all over Wolf's hard muscled and rippled back and ass, and he liked oiling me up as well. Of course, we also had plenty of volunteers to add more oil anytime that either of us felt that we needed more. The sensations of lying comfortably on side by side massage tables by the poolside, listening to Wolf moan with pleasure as the still sore muscles of his rock hard back and shoulders were expertly worked over by a tall, blonde Scandinavian masseur, while a handsome Asian boy massaged me at the same time, was surprisingly erotic, especially when both of us were sucked off by the naked, muscular boys giving us the massages as a finish to our total body rubdowns!

We both had plenty of sex, all of it safe, both with each other and with a lot of the other guests at the ranch, as we seemed to be the best built couple there, and we were the objects of a lot of desire and fantasies.

On the first night we went back to the torture barn after Wolf's torture by the horses, Donald got his chance to practice his flogging technique on Wolf's back. When he had worked on Wolf's back for about ten minutes, and seemed to be confident of his ability to use a flogger correctly, he asked me if I would give him permission to suck my slave off while he was still bound to the whipping post outside of the barn.

I told him that it would be all right with me, so Donald immediately dropped to his knees in front of my helpless, sweat dripping slave boy, and sucked his cock until, with a loud groan of pleasure, Wolf shot a thick load into his mouth.

We spent a lot of time in the torture barn the next few nights. I stretched both Chuck and Jimmy, his lover, on facing St. Andrew's crosses in the barn, and made both of them watch each other being tortured by me with Wolf's help.

I had the pleasure of being served by the twin brother slaves as their reward for helping to torture Wolf's nipples during the torture by the horses. Their black master worked on Wolf by strapping him into a sling and fucking him slowly but forcefully with his thick, ebony cock while working Wolf's tits with his strong fingers. He shot a thick load of cum all over my helpless slave's hard chest, which was then licked off by his twin slaves, who were lifeguards and local surfing champions from San Diego. Their tall, powerfully muscled master, as it turned out, was a drill instructor from the Marine Corps training base there.

One of my hottest memories of the ranch was lying on one of the lounges by the pool, while two hot young men alternated sucking my cock and balls, while two more guys worked on my nipples and pits with their mouths, while all the while; Wolf had his cock in my mouth, fucking it! It was almost too much pleasure to bear, especially when Wolf shot his load deeply into my throat at almost the same time I came in the mouths of the two guys sucking me, and the two men working on my nipples jacked off across my pecs and then licked each other's cum from my chest!

I got to inflict my fifteen minutes, and then some, of torture on Donald's slave Jay, as I still owed him for hurting Wolf's nipples the first night we were there. Donald told me that Jay had been inspired by watching Wolf endure the tortures that I had subjected him to, and Jay was determined to expand his own limits of endurance.

I stretched him spread-eagled upside down on one of the jail cell doors leaning on the wall of the barn, suspending him by his ankles from the top of the door, and stretching his arms down and out to the bottom corners. I then gave his tightly stretched chest, his washboard abdominal muscles, and his rippling ribcage a good hard flogging, followed with fucking his mouth until, with Donald's permission, I shot a thick, hard load of cum into his mouth and forced him to swallow my load. Wolf then followed by sucking and chewing Jay's flat, pink nipples with his teeth and fucking his mouth and feeding him another hot load of cum. Donald was so turned on by watching his boy being tortured, that he asked me for instructions on how to whip his boy. I showed him how to work a single tail whip properly, which was a different technique than using a flogger, then watched as he worked on his howling, writhing slave, whipping his already tender chest and abs until they were covered with livid, red welts. Donald had to shove his cock into Jay's mouth to quiet him after his whipping was finished, then fucked his mouth until he shot, forcing Jay to swallow his third load of sperm within thirty minutes! Donald then jacked Jay's cock off until his slave shot a thick, creamy load of cum into his hand. He then forced Jay to lap up his own sperm, for his fourth load, hanging upside down the entire time!

I looked at Wolf and softly said; "God, I think we've created a monster!" Wolf snickered at that. He then leaned in and whispered in my ear; "It's aliiiive!" in his best Boris Karloff lisp. I had the hardest time keeping from laughing out loud at that!

Finally, after several nights of uninhibited sexual pleasure, and days of recreation like horseback riding and mountain biking, we came to the last night that we were going to be at the ranch. I don't think Wolf had any idea of what was going to happen to him that night, as I had only told Chuck, and he had agreed to keep it a secret. The whole evening started when Chuck made an announcement at dinner that something special was planned for that night at ten in the barn, and that everyone should plan to attend.

Wolf looked at me and asked; "Are we going to be there, Sir?"

I smiled to myself as I told him; "I guess we'll show up, boy. I don't want to disappoint anyone."

Later that night, as we were getting ready to go to the barn, I gathered Wolf in my arms and told him again that I was so proud of everything he had endured at the ranch and in the time that we had been together. I also told him that tonight was going to be special. At that, I think he began to suspect that something extraordinary was going to happen, but he had no idea what! When we left to go to the barn that night, Wolf was dressed in his cutoffs and combat boots, but no shirt, as usual, with his hair pulled back in a thick ponytail and a bandanna around his head as a headband. I put his wide, studded slave collar back around his throat and locked it in position, telling him that he was back in full slave mode for the night, since it was going to be our last night at the ranch, and I wanted it to be memorable. I was wearing my leather jeans and my sleeveless denim shirt, with my vest over it, and my knee-high logger boots. Wolf's arms were empty for a change, as his wrists were locked together behind his back with padlocks on his wide leather wrist restraints, but I was carrying a wrapped package I had retrieved from its hiding place in the trunk of the Chevy. We arrived at the barn a few minutes after ten, and when we walked in, all the lights were off except for a single spotlight focused on a bondage table standing vertically in the middle of the floor. Wolf looked a bit confused at the scene, and I gave him a wicked grin. I briefly stopped to see Chuck, and hand him the package I was carrying, and then walked directly into the circle of light next to the table and turned towards the men gathered in the shadows of the barn.

"Gentlemen, your attention please! We are here to celebrate one of the most important events in the life of a slave-boy. Wolf, step up here please!"

Wolf looked totally confused as he walked up in front of me, and dropped to his knees in his usual posture of submission, but then the light of understanding dawned in his eyes, and he gave me a slow smile and bent down and began to lick my boots.

The guys watching us murmured softly as he worked the shiny black leather with his tongue, until I ordered him back up onto his knees.

"This is my slave, Carlos Greywolf, better known to a lot of you as just Wolf. He has been my slave for over a year and he has never failed to surpass my expectations. He has endured tortures and suffering beyond the range of most men, as some of you have witnessed over the last few days, and has never complained. His strength and his loyalty are unquestioned, and I hope he knows just how much I truly love him!"

At that, Wolf looked up into my deep, blue eyes, with his soft brown eyes brimming with tears, and softly said; "I do, Sir. And I love you, too, Sir!"

I told him to stand and turn around as I unlocked his wrist restraints from each other, and called for Chuck to bring me the package that I had handed him. He stepped up and gave me the package and whispered in my ear; "You are the luckiest bastard on earth to have him!"

I whispered back; "Tell me something I don't already know!" Chuck just grinned and winked at me.

I turned to Wolf and told him; "To celebrate your service and your love, I present you with a gift from your master to his slave!"

I handed him the package and watched the expression on his face turn from curiosity to total shock as he unwrapped a pair of custom made chaps in shining black leather! He turned to me, his face glowing as the smell of the fresh leather wafted into the air. Wolf had never owned any leathers of his own, as I was from the old school that felt that a slave had to earn the right to wear leather, but Wolf had certainly earned that right in the time he had been with me! I just held him in my arms as he finally broke down, and began sobbing with happiness into my chest. I held him until he calmed down, and then loudly told him; "Well, boy, there goes your reputation as a tough bottom."

A wave of laughter went through the group of guys watching us. I told Wolf; "Well, don't just stand there, boy. Drop the shorts and try them on!"

Wolf immediately unfastened his cut-offs and let them drop to the floor. His cock bounced upright, as he was totally turned on by all the attention. He stepped into the legs of the chaps one at a time and worked the waistband up. I knelt in front of him and pulled the zippers on the legs down to his boots. Wolf fastened the snaps on the front of the waist, and I stepped behind him to pull the thongs in the back of the waist tight. I tied them off, and quickly admired how the leather framed the perfect twin globes of his firm, hairless golden brown ass.

I was relieved to see that the legs of the chaps fit him as well as I hoped they would, clinging to his sculpted thighs and calves like a second skin. He turned towards the guys watching, and there was an audible murmur in the crowd at the sight of his deeply tanned, ripped and shredded muscular body highlighted by the black leather chaps, whose color was echoed by Wolf's thick mane of raven black hair, the studded leather slave collar locked around his throat, and the leather cock ring around the base of his thick, hard dick.

We heard one guy exclaim; "God damn, what a stud!" At that, the whole group began to applaud and whistle!

Wolf turned to me with the happiest expression I had ever seen on his face, hugged me, and whispered into my ear; "Oh God, Sir! Thank you, Thank you!"

I told him; "We're not done yet, boy!"

I held up my hand to signal the guys watching for silence, and then faced Wolf and loudly asked him; "Boy, what is your all-time desire? The one thing you want more than anything else?"

He unhesitatingly answered; "I want to be permanently marked as your property, Sir. I want everyone to know that I belong to you, and you alone, Sir!"

I answered; "Good answer, boy, because tonight you are going to get your wish! Now, boy, get on that table and prepare yourself for extreme pain!"

Wolf immediately stepped backwards against the upright bondage table. He put his feet on the lip that extended from the bottom of the table, and stood upright with his back against the table. I knelt down and began to use the leather straps attached to the table to bind my slave firmly. By the time I was done, Wolf was totally immobilized against the table with straps fastened tightly across his ankles, knees, waist, biceps, forearms, wrists, and across his neck. His arms were strapped down next to his sides, causing his pecs to bulge out.

I rotated the table back, so that Wolf was now at about a forty-five degree angle to the floor. His thick, bronzed chest rose and fell with his breathing, glistening in the light of the spotlight shining down on him. I worked on his thick tits with my fingers and my mouth for about five minutes, to make sure his nipples were fully erect and hard.

Finally, I asked him; "Are you ready for this, boy?"

He smiled at me; "Oh yes, Sir! I've been ready for this for over a year, Sir!"

I turned and signaled to Chuck, who wheeled in a cart usually used to carry trays of hot food in the kitchen. Only now, it was carrying a small charcoal burner like a hibachi, filled with glowing coals. Sticking out of the coals was the handles of the branding irons I had had fabricated months ago. Each of the irons had a short wooden handle with four evenly spaced thin metal rods sticking out of one end. The rods ran together for about six inches, and then spread out to surround a flat metal ring. The ring was just big enough in diameter to fit around one of Wolf's thick, pumped nipples. Where each of the rods was attached to the ring, there was a small, elongated triangle of metal welded to the ring. The total effect was that the mark that ring would leave on Wolf's chest was rather like an old-fashioned compass rose, a circle with a point on all four sides.

Wolf moaned loudly when he saw the red-hot irons in the glowing coals. He knew that he was in for some of the most severe pain he had ever had to endure! The burning of his cockhead had been bad enough, but this time he knew he was going to have to endure two separate burnings in one torture session. Unsurprisingly, however, his cock, which had softened, immediately started to swell again, until it was fully hard.

I took off my vest and shirt, leaving me stripped to the waist, my skin starting to shine with sweat from the heat of the coals in the hibachi on the cart next to the table. I pulled on a pair of work gloves to protect my hands. The handles were wood, but they were still pretty hot. At a nod from me, Chuck stepped up to the table and began to pump the coals with a small hand bellows used in the horseshoeing shop.

Wolf moaned again in anticipation and there was a murmur from the crowd watching when I pulled one of the irons from the coals and saw that it was glowing a deep cherry red. I set it back in the coals and a hush fell over the crowd when I turned to Wolf.

"Carlos Greywolf, In the presence of all these men who are gathered here tonight, do you fully and freely submit to the permanent marking of your body? Do you give yourself to me, Eric Kurtz, for the rest of your life as my slave, and my property, to do with as I see fit, body, soul, heart and mind?"

Wolf looked directly into my eyes as he answered; "Yes, Sir! My body is yours to do whatever you want to! You already have my heart and soul, my Master! I love you with all my mind, and I give myself to you fully and of my own free will as your slave for the rest of my life, Sir!"

I asked him; "Do you want both at once, or do you want me to do one nipple at a time? Your choice, boy."

Wolf immediately answered; "Sir, please do both at the same time, Sir!"

At that, I leaned in and kissed Wolf deeply and passionately. We held the kiss for a few seconds. I whispered in Wolf's ear; "I love you more than anything else in the world, boy! Now, get ready!"

Wolf just nodded, his eyes full of tears. I stepped back and picked up both irons. They were glowing red, and smoking lightly. I held them out over Wolf's chest, adjusting them so the patterns of the brands would be even, and then I told him; "Take a deep breath and hold it, boy!"

My slave's massive chest expanded to its fullest, and then he flexed his pecs rock hard. I made the final adjustments, and then pressed the glowing irons against his chest!

Wolf's body immediately slammed against the restraints as every muscle in his body convulsed in raw, shrieking, total agony and flexed to their ultimate limits, the veins and tendons popping out on every rock-hard muscle in his sculpted physique. As I held the irons on his chest, I could hear the sizzling sound of the red-hot metal burning into his pectoral muscles and could smell the burning flesh. The smoke rose from my slave's chest as I marked him for the rest of his life!

Wolf held himself silent for a few seconds, his teeth gritted tightly, and his eyes squeezed shut, the cords and tendons bulging in his neck. Then, a scream of raw agony was torn from his throat!

He shrieked; "OH SHIT, SIR, OH SHIT! OH, FUCK YES! TORTURE ME, SIR! MARK ME FOR LIFE, MASTER!! MAKE ME YOUR SLAVE FOREVER!! I LOVE YOU, MASTER!! AAAAUUUGGGGHHH!!!"

I held the irons on his chest for a good fifteen seconds; Wolf screaming for the entire time, to insure deep brandings that wouldn't fade over time.

Finally, I pulled the irons away. The angry red marks on Wolf's chest were perfectly positioned, the rings surrounding his nipples with the four points perfectly aligned.

I dropped the irons onto the cart and leaned over Wolf. His eyes were closed tightly, his handsome face contorted in agony, his entire body shaking and shuddering uncontrollably. I reached out and stroked my hand down his cheek. When he didn't respond, I gently slapped his cheek to get through to him. I had to slap him three or four times before he relaxed a little and opened his eyes. Wolf stared wildly about for a few seconds, his chest heaving, before his bloodshot eyes focused on me.

"It's O. K. boy, it's O. K. It's over. You did good, boy" I comforted him. In front of everyone watching, I bent down and took Wolf's throbbing cock into my mouth. I only had to suck it for a moment before, with a groan, Wolf shot a huge load of sperm into my mouth!

I swallowed his load as fast as I could, before standing back up and kissing Wolf deeply. I then looked into his eyes and comforted him softly until his breathing calmed back down to normal. There were tears running down Wolf's face as I rotated the table to its fully horizontal position, and began to remove the restraints from his body. When I had totally released my pain-wracked slave from his bondage, I asked him if he was capable of standing back up by himself, or if he needed a while longer to recover from his ordeal.

He softly replied; "Sir, I don't think I can stand up just yet. I still feel kind of shaky."

I picked up my shirt and folded it into a pillow, and put it under his head. I then softly told him; "Just take as long as you need, boy. I'll be right here for you!"

As Wolf calmed down, Chuck turned the lights in the barn back up to their normal level, and dimmed the spotlight over the bondage table. Some of the other guys, including Donald and Jay, came up and asked if Wolf was all right, and complimented Wolf on his incredible strength and endurance. I thanked them all for their words of support, and assured them that he just needed a few minutes to recover before I took him back to our cabin to dress his burns.

One of the other guys, with tears streaming down his face, said that this was the most erotic and sensual scene he had ever witnessed, because it was done in the spirit of pure love between a master and his slave!

After about ten minutes, with me stroking and comforting him the entire time, Wolf asked me to help him back to the cabin. As I rotated the table to its upright position, a hush fell over the barn as almost all the other activity stopped. As Wolf stepped down onto the floor, while I held his arm for support, the other guys began to applaud my slave! I leaned into him, and wrapped my arm around his shoulders for support and held him tight as he swayed a bit, before straightening up.

He turned to me and whispered into my ear; “So help me, if you say ’They like us’ again, I’ll smack you!” He then winked at me and gave me his crooked smile. Right there, I knew he was going to be all right! He was gently teasing me, the way I had done to him so many times before.

I just gave him my best innocent look, and said; “Who, me? It never crossed my mind!”

Wolf just gave me his “Yeah, Right!” look as we walked out of the barn and slowly walked to our cabin, where I gently cleaned his burned pecs and dressed his brands with sterile gauze pads as I had been taught to do by my doctor. I then put him in his own bed, where he could sleep undisturbed by me. I knew Wolf had earned a good night’s sleep, and also, this night he had earned my undying love and respect. Any lingering doubts about Wolf had been totally and fully eliminated by our stay at the ranch. He was the perfect slave, and the love of my life, and would remain so until the day I died!

Chapter Eleven
Eric's Story

The next day dawned rather misty and cloudy, so I knew we would be going back to Sausalito with the top up on the car. I walked Wolf over to the dining room for breakfast, where we exchanged phone numbers and e-mail addresses with a lot of the guys there.

After settling up with Chuck and promising to come back soon, we headed back home.

As I drove, Wolf just tried to relax. I had changed the dressings on his chest just before we left, but I knew it was going to be a long, slow, and probably painful time of healing for him. The events of the last week had taken my handsome slave-boy lover to the edge of his strength and endurance, and maybe just a bit beyond.

After about a half hour or so, Wolf said; "Sir, do you remember when you said that someday you would tell me about how you became a top man? I'd really like to know, if you want to tell me," I looked over at him and decided he had earned the right to know about my past, since it looked like we would be spending the rest of our lives together.

"O.K. boy, I'll tell you, but you have to tell me how you became the pain-happy muscle boy that I've come to know and love!"

Wolf gave me his crooked grin and said; "Fair enough. You first, though."

I shot back; "Oh great, another pushy bottom!"

We both laughed at that, but then we got serious as I started to tell Wolf my story.

"I was living in the bay area, going to school and enjoying myself, as a lot of young, gay men did at their first time living away from family. My parents were still home in Indiana, where my father owned and ran a successful software development company. I was going to school in Silicon Valley, to develop my software writing and program development skills. It was an ideal life for me, as I had lots of friends, and I was exploring my newfound love of the leather lifestyle."

"The problem started the summer my parents flew out to visit me for my twenty second birthday and see how my life and schooling were going. I had decided to tell them I was gay, as I had never come out to them. I wasn't sure how the would take it, being from a conservative, Catholic background in the Midwest."

"My dad flew out in his private plane, since flying was his hobby, and he was a good pilot. When they arrived, we had a good visit until the last night they were here, when I finally told them about my lifestyle. Unfortunately, they didn't take it as well as I had hoped they would, and we had a major fight. My mom was more supportive than my father, but I could still see the disapproval in her face. We had a rather awkward parting at the airport, but at least my parents said I could come home whenever I wanted to and we would talk about my life. They told me that they loved me but were shocked at my 'choice' of lifestyle."

"Sadly, that visit never got to happen, as I received a phone call in the middle of that night, telling me that dad's plane had gone missing somewhere in the middle of the Rocky Mountains. I tell you, I went through hell for about three days, until I got the call telling me that searchers had found the wreckage, and that there were no survivors."

Wolf looked at me with tears brimming in his eyes and said; "I'm really sorry about that, Sir. I kind of went through the same thing when I lost my parents in the car crash, but I knew about it almost immediately. I can't imagine having to wait to find out!"

I looked back at him and said; "The worst part was knowing that we parted under such bad feelings and we never got to sort it all out!" I had to take a few deep breaths to compose myself before I continued with my story.

"As you could imagine, I felt like hell for weeks afterward. I don't have any brothers or sisters, and both of my parents were only children, so I had absolutely no close family other than my parents. I really went into a private rage for a while and started to really fuck up my life. I was doing lots of drugs, and drinking a lot, hoping it would help. It didn't! Things were so bad that I don't even remember a thing about the funeral service and memorial services. I was totally in shock, and I was pretty fucked up during the whole trip back to Indy."

By now, tears were running down Wolf's cheeks. His only comment was; "Oh shit, Sir."

"Yeah-oh shit indeed! Finally it came to the night that I was in a bar on Folsom and finally went totally postal. I don't remember anything about it, but

I was told afterward that I totally freaked out in the bar and tried to interfere in a scene. All I knew for sure was when I woke up I was in a dark room tied naked and spread-eagled to a cross. I tried to holler for help, but then I discovered I was gagged and couldn't do a thing. I also had the worst hangover in my life. I think I would have had to feel better to die!"

"Finally, after about what could have been ten minutes, or could have been an hour, I heard the door open and a figure walked into the room. All I could see was that it was a man in leathers It was too dark to see anything else."

"He looked at me and said; 'Well, I see you're finally awake, boy.' That was all. I had no idea where I was or who he was, or what was going to happen. That's about the most frightened I've ever been in my life. Or I thought it was, until he turned up the lights, and I saw I was bound in a really well equipped torture chamber!"

Wolf gave me a small smile, and said; "Trust me, Sir, I know the feeling!"

I looked at him, and with a wry grin said; 'More than you know, boy. It's the same dungeon!"

Wolf's eyes widened as he breathed; "No shit, Sir. Really?"

"Yeah, really! Where we live now was originally his house. Anyway, the man, whose name I found out later was Michael, just stood there and looked at me. I couldn't shake the feeling I had seen him somewhere before, but at the time I wasn't in any shape to think about it."

"Finally, he spoke again and said; 'Not so tough now, are you slave?'"

"I had absolutely no idea of what he was talking about, and what had happened to me that night. All I could do was look at him, and hope that he wasn't going to kill me."

"He looked at me and said; 'You don't have the faintest idea of what happened, or what you did, do you boy?' When I didn't respond to him, he grabbed a cat-o-nine tails and gave me about five hard lashes across my chest.

He snarled, "First lesson, boy! When I ask you a question, you'd better answer!"

Then he leaned in close and asked again; 'You don't know, do you, boy?' This time I shook my head, even though it felt like my brains were detached and were rattling loose inside my skull.

"That's better" he growled at me. Even the sound of his voice sent shivers down my spine. It was a low bass rumble that seemed to hold menace with every word. He reached out and began to twist my nipples as he told me; "I hope you're really as tough as you made out in the bar last night, because we're gonna find out if you are!"

"He wasn't a very tall man, but he was really powerfully built. I was in good shape, but I could tell that trying to fight my way out of there would be totally futile. Besides, when you're bound hand and foot to a St. Andrew's cross, there's not a whole hell of a lot you can do!"

Wolf just gave me one of his crooked grins and said; "Well, Duh! Preaching to the choir here, Sir!" I gave him a mock glare, but I couldn't hold it, and it turned into a grin.

"Next, Michael pulled out some more various cats and floggers, and then proceeded to give me the most intense flogging I had ever endured on my chest and stomach. By the time it was done, I was screaming into my gag, and felt like I was on the verge of either passing out or throwing up from the pain. I would never have believed that one person's body could endure that level of suffering. That is, until I met you, of course!"

Wolf actually blushed at that!

"Anyway, when he put down the last of the floggers that he used on me, I couldn't do a thing except hang there on the cross, trying to breathe and hoping that the torture was done, but somehow knowing that it wasn't! Michael then stepped in front of me, now stripped to the waist with the sweat running down his muscles, and unfastened the gag from around my head."

"As soon as he pulled it from my mouth, I made the mistake of hollering; 'Who the fuck are you? Let me out of here! I'm gonna kill you when I get loose, you bastard!' His only response was a solid slap to my face that made my already aching head feel like it was going to fall off!"

"A little respect to your master, boy!" He snarled at me. "I own your sorry, drunken ass now, and the sooner you recognize that, the better off you'll be!"

Being the smart-ass that I was at the time, I just hollered back at him; "Nobody owns me, you son-of-a-bitch! Let me out of here! This is kidnapping! You're gonna spend the rest of your life in jail, you bastard!"

"This time, his response was a solid slap to the other side of my face! Then he leaned in close to me and snapped; 'You wanna call the cops, slave? I'll save you the trouble!' He reached into the pocket of his leather pants and pulled out his wallet and flipped it open, showing me his San Francisco Police badge!"

Wolf gasped; "Oh shit, he was a cop, Sir?"

I grinned at him; "Oooh yeah! But, that was only the first of many surprises Mike had for me!"

"To make a long story short, Mike kept me chained up in the dungeon for over a week, feeding me and letting me sleep when he was at work, but otherwise he worked me over almost constantly when he was home. It came out that I had tried to break into the middle of a scene in the bar, drunk off my ass, bragging that I could do everything better than the top who was working over his slave!"

Wolf grimaced; "Ouch! Not too bright, Sir."

"Yeah- no shit. Anyway it turns out that Mike was the officer who responded to the call from the bartender about the disturbance I had caused. He was actually off duty and on his way home when the call came in on the police scanner in his car. He was still in uniform and the bartender was a friend of his, so when Mike told him that he would take care of me, the bartender called the police back and told them that the problem had been resolved and that they didn't need to send anyone out. Mike told me later that he had slapped a pair of handcuffs on me when I tried to punch him out, but that I was so drunk that I missed and actually fell flat on my face in the middle of the bar! He also told me later that he had seen me a few times in the bar and had been attracted to me, but since I had a real attitude problem whenever he tried to talk to me, that he never followed up on his attraction."

I gave Wolf a rueful smile and said; "I guess I was the living example of the old saying- instant asshole-just add alcohol. Now you know why I drink very little in a bar and none at all anywhere else. I wasn't really a true alcoholic, but I was well on my way to being one."

"Anyway, after about a week of being kept prisoner in Mike's dungeon and being constantly tortured, I just couldn't take anymore. I was just a huge mass of welts and bruises from constant whippings and floggings, and other tortures. So, one day when he came down into the dungeon after getting off work, I just broke down, and started crying and begging him to let me go. I was really surprised when he released me from my bonds and sat down on the bed I was on, wrapped his arms around me, and just held me while I cried myself out. When I was done, he looked into my eyes and gently asked; 'Are you ready to listen to me now, Eric? I've been waiting for you to come to your senses.'"

"He gave me a smile that was surprisingly gentle and said; 'You know, you're either really tough, or you're really stubborn!'"

"That really surprised me, because I hadn't told him my name, and I didn't know that he knew who I was. I just told him that I wanted to know what was going on and where I was!"

"Mike said that he knew that he was taking a risk holding me prisoner like he was, that he could be charged with kidnapping and various other charges if I wanted to be a bastard about the situation, but he was betting I wouldn't do it after he explained what he was doing."

"I looked at him and just said; 'Start explaining!' I was thoroughly pissed off at him, but was just too physically exhausted to do anything about it."

"He sat back and told me; 'I was one of the officers that did part of the investigation of your parent's crash at the airport. We had to do it because it was where the flight originated. I'm really sorry about your parents, by the way.' At that I just started to cry again, but this time it was from the realization that they were really gone. Mike just held me for a while longer, until I calmed down again, and then he continued his explanation."

"'In the investigation, I found out that they were your family, and I wanted to see how you were holding up. When I saw that you were falling apart, I decided to try to help you any way I could, since I knew who you were and I had always thought you were a smart guy, as well as drop dead handsome.' He smiled at me then, seemingly a little embarrassed at his admission."

Wolf smiled at me and said; "Well, he got that part right, Sir. You are drop dead handsome. But then again, I'm just a little biased, Sir!"

I smiled at him and then continued; "Mike told me he wasn't sure what to do to help me until he heard the call about the bar disturbance on his scanner and stopped to see if he could help, even though he was off duty. When he saw that I was the cause of the problem, it was then that he decided to essentially kidnap me to keep me out of any more trouble. He then told me that with the help of some friends in the city hall, he had arranged for me to essentially disappear from the city for a while. I had been moved out of my apartment and all my belongings were in storage and were safe, and I was taking a semester off from college to deal with my loss."

"I looked at him and asked; 'Well, now what?' He said that over the next few months, he was going to continue my slave training, and that I would be living with him."

"My first reaction was; 'Fuck you, are you nuts? I'm no slave!' Mike grabbed my hair, yanked my head back, and snarled at me; 'You are now, boy!' He then kissed me harder and more passionately then anyone else had ever done until then. In the middle of the kiss, I suddenly realized what he was risking for me, and what he could be giving up for me, his job and even his freedom if I had him arrested, and a feeling of happiness came over me that hadn't felt for quite a while. I wrapped my arms around him and held on like a drowning man would hold on to a piece of driftwood, because I realized that I truly was drowning in my self-pity and anger!"

Wolf was watching me with tears running down his face which were matched by the tears streaking down my own face at the memories of Mike. I gave him a twisted grin and said; "Aren't we a pair of tough leather men?"

Wolf said; "Hey, I was fine until you started crying, Sir!"

I just gave him a sideways glare and muttered; Yeah, right!"

Wolf gave me his familiar lopsided smile and wiped his face. Then he leaned over and gave me a kiss, and then leaned back in his seat with a slight groan, as his chest muscles worked around his fresh brandings.

Shortly thereafter, we stopped at a small restaurant to get lunch and take a break from driving. As I walked around a bit to stretch my legs, I realized how difficult it was to tell the story of my past to anyone, even the love of my life. I was always rather private about my personal life, so this was hard for me to do. But, at the same time I felt it would help me if someone else knew my story, and I couldn't think of anyone else I would rather tell it to than Wolf.

After we started back home, I continued my story, telling Wolf; "After admitting to myself that I really needed someone in my life, I accepted Mike's offer to train me as his slave. It turned out that he was really knowledgeable about the whole leather culture and lifestyle. He had been trained by an old school New York City top, and so he was passing on his acquired knowledge and training to me, much as I hope to do to you."

Wolf smiled at me and said; "I can't think of anyone else I'd rather learn from, Sir." Then he got serious when he said; "I know that Mike passed away, Sir. How did that happen?"

I had to think and compose myself for a moment before I could tell Wolf; "Mike died about four years ago after a long battle with AIDS. It was the hardest thing I've ever had to do in my life, watching this strong, vital, healthy man turn into a wasted shell. That's one of the main reasons I insist that we both get tested every six months, and why we don't have unprotected anal sex with anyone other than each other. Why do you think I won't let you take most guys' loads in your mouth, boy? I want you around for as long as possible!"

Wolf looked solemnly at me for a moment and then said; "I really appreciate that, Sir. I know sometimes it might not seem so, or sometimes I really want some hot guys load in my mouth, but I know that you have rules against that. I just never knew exactly why. And, I don't think I've ever thanked you for looking out for me that way."

I just smiled at him and said; "I just want you around for a long, long time, boy. You're sooo much fun to torture. And incidentally, I happen to really love you, boy!"

Wolf slid over on the seat and snuggled up next to me, and with tears in his eyes, said; "Trust me, Sir, the feeling is mutual!"

We drove on in silence for a while, just listening to the rhythm of the wipers before Wolf asked; "How long were you a slave to Mike, before he started to train you as a top, Sir?"

"I was a pure slave for about two years, before he decided that I had matured enough and had grasped the seriousness of the mindset involved in being a master. Then, over the next couple of years, I slowly started to get experience in being a serious top. I started by topping Mike in some scenes at home, with him critiquing my performance, before we would start picking up guys in the bars and take turns topping them."

Wolf grinned and said; "Woof-What a fantasy that would be! To be tied up and tortured by both you and the man who trained you. Wow! I never had anyone to train me as a slave before you, Sir. My first experiences with being tied up and tortured were with friends as a kid, and an older cousin in Arizona, but I never had a real master before you, Sir!"

I smiled back and told him; Well, there were a lot of guys who felt the same way, but there were also a lot who just couldn't deal with two tops."

Wolf smiled impishly; "Wimps! At least I could take being worked over by both you and Chuck, Sir!"

I smiled at Wolf and told him; "I know that I told you that I was proud of the way you endured being tortured by the both of us, but I want you to know that I really meant it. I speak from painful personal experience, that enduring two-on-one torture is really hard, and I'm really proud of you!"

Wolf smiled at me and said; "If it had been anyone else, I'm not sure I would have tried to endure that much pain. That was the most I've ever taken, but for you, I'd have endured anything. I knew you wouldn't let anything happen to me, Sir!"

About this time, we started to get into heavier traffic heading back into the bay area, being a Sunday afternoon, so I told Wolf I would finish telling him about my past after we got home. I needed to concentrate on driving, since the weather had gotten worse since we had left the ranch. I drove on the rest of the way home in silence, just listening to the sounds of the rain drumming on the top of the car, and the beat of the wipers, both of us lost in our own thoughts of the past.

Chapter Twelve
Mike

After working our way through the bay area traffic to Sausalito, we finally arrived home, tired from the drive and the activities of the previous week at the ranch, but happy to be home. I could feel that the relationship between Wolf and myself had undergone a quantum shift, but in a good way. I felt that our bond of love, not to mention our relationship as master and slave, had been strengthened to the point that it couldn't be broken. At least, I hoped it couldn't be broken!

I told Wolf to go inside and relax while I unloaded he car, as he wasn't really up to doing too much with his still sore, freshly branded chest. I fixed us some dinner and then we both changed into casual clothes. I put fresh dressings on Wolf's nipples after a long, relaxing soak in the hot tub. Unfortunately, Wolf could only sit on one of the seats in the tub up to his waist, as he had to keep his dressings as dry as possible for the first few days. Neither one of us wanted to do too much else after our long drive, and a very tiring week at the ranch.

Later that night, while we were watching some really bad television movie, Wolf asked me if I would continue telling him about my past.

I turned off the television, leaned back in the corner of the couch, and told Wolf to sit down between my legs. I wrapped my arms around him and pulled him back against me, nuzzling the back of his neck and enjoying the clean smell of his hair and skin, and the feel of his hard back against my chest. I sat for a few moments, collecting my thoughts and listening to the rain continuing to fall, punctuated by the occasional rumble of thunder, and then continued telling him my story.

"I guess I had gotten to the part where Mike had started to let me top other guys as well as himself. It was a real eye-opener to see what I had been doing wrong while trying to be a top before. I had always thought that I could do all the things that a top does to his bottom boy, even though I hadn't had most of them done to me. I had never known that to be a really good top, one has to be a bottom first, so you know exactly what something feels likes to the other person. It also helps to be able to tell when your bottom is in some form of distress, or is having an endorphin overload, and you need to stop the scene, even though the bottom seems to be all right. You'd be amazed how often that can happen!"

Wolf turned and smiled at me and said; "Well then, I ought to make a really good top someday, since there hasn't been too much you haven't done to me yet and I really know what an endorphin hit feels like!"

I just gave him an evil smile, and said: "You'd be surprised what I haven't done to you yet, boy. Besides, what makes you think I'll ever let you go to become someone's top? You're my slave for life, boy. Or, are you thinking of leaving me someday?"

Wolf turned to me with a shocked look on his face, which slid into a grin when he saw the wicked smile I gave him.

He laughed and said; "You had me going there for a minute, Sir! I've never thought of leaving you. You're my master for life, Sir, just like I promised at the ranch. As for what you haven't done to me yet, I can hardly wait, Sir!"

I smiled to myself and told him; "Watch it, boy. Sometimes you get exactly what you wish for. You never know what I might have up my sleeve next."

He moaned softly; "Threaten me with a good time, Sir."

I laughed again and continued my story. "Anyway, I worked as a top man with Mike in three way and even four way scenes for a year or so before topping on my own more and more often. I knew that my reputation was starting to recover from my bouts of drinking and drugs, when I started to get asked to do demos and assist in shows at various bars on Folsom, and in the Castro district, and that's when I discovered that I was as much of an exhibitionist as I am. It used to be so much fun working on various guys in the different bars on club nights. That's one of the reasons that I love to work you over in the backrooms of some of the bars we go to. I love showing you off for the crowds almost as much as you love showing off yourself."

"The downside came when I had to start going out by myself to the bars more and more as Mike started to show the symptoms of full-blown AIDS. He insisted that I needed to keep going out as much as I could, because he knew he wouldn't be around much longer. I had known he was positive since we had met, of course, and we always had safe sex, but I didn't expect how badly he was going to deteriorate, and how quickly, once it started. It really hurt me to see Mike start to waste away, since he was the person who had gotten me really interested in serious bodybuilding, as he was the San Francisco P.D. champion and had won several other competitions in the state as well. However, since he had started to feel bad, I went to the gym alone, as well. He insisted I needed to keep on training and working out as well. He told me that he expected me to be a champion just like he had been. It made me feel good when I won my first competition even though it was after Mike couldn't work out anymore. However, he was in the crowd, cheering me on!"

Wolf turned to me and said; "That had to be hard, Sir. Watching someone you really care about go downhill like that."

"Believe me, boy, it was." I said in a shaky voice.

We sat silently for a while, as I had to try to regain my composure, which I started to lose thinking back on the long period of decline Mike went through. I drew strength from Wolf's quiet support, though.

Finally, Wolf turned back to me and said; "Sir, if this is too hard, I can wait to hear any more of your story. It's all right, I understand."

I shook my head. "No, I think I need to tell it to someone. I've kept this to myself for far too long and I can't think of anyone else who deserves more to know the truth about me than the man I want to spend the rest of my life with."

Wolf smiled, leaned in and kissed me and said; "Thank you, Sir. I appreciate the honor, and I want you to know that I feel the same way about you, too."

I continued; "I knew that Mike cared about me, not just as a slave boy, but also as a lover and a friend, and I loved him because he probably saved my life. I would have drunken myself to death or overdosed on drugs, or something else, if not for Mike. He gave me a new sense of responsibility for my own life. I had just about given up on myself because of the way my parents and I parted. I had never quite shaken the feeling of being responsible for the accident. I had always thought that my dad was in such a hurry to get away from me, that he took a chance and flew when he shouldn't have!"

Wolf softly moaned, "Oh God, Sir."

"Over the course of time, however, Mike convinced me that this simply wasn't so. His investigation as part of the police report showed that the weather was perfect when my parents flew out, but an unexpected storm system caught everyone, even the weather service, by surprise."

I gave Wolf a sad smile and told him; "I like torturing other guys, but self torture, especially mental self torture, isn't any fun at all."

"Mike did other things for me as well. As I mentioned, the house that we live in was originally his. He was left the house by his parents, and after we were together for a while, he changed his will and left the house to me, even though I had plenty of money of my own that was left me by both of my parents once we got the estate and probate taken care of. I've never told you exactly how much I was left by my parents, since I wasn't totally sure about our future together until this last week, but I'm currently worth somewhere in the vicinity of 85 or 90 million dollars. That includes stock in the company, land in Indiana and here in California, and other things like the first five cars in the car collection. Dad liked classic Chevys, so that's why I have so many of them. That's why I spend a couple of hours every morning working on the computer while you are doing your chores. I'm dealing with the daily business that the board of directors of my dad's company back in Indiana need me to deal with, since I'm now the majority stockholder in the company."

Wolf looked at me in total shock, before he said; "My God! Sir, I really didn't know, but I want you to know that it really doesn't make that much difference to me. I would love you even if you were just making a regular amount of money and I had to work as well." I smiled at him and gave him another hug, and then continued;

"Mike also insisted that I had to go back to school and finish getting my degree in software design. I had an incentive to study that probably no one else in the history of the school had. Any time I had a grade point average that dropped below a 3.5, I had to spend several hours in the dungeon enduring some of the worst tortures I could ever imagine. Believe you me, I really buckled down and worked my ass off in school, and graduated first in my class!" Wolf laughed at that.

I chuckled softly as another random memory crossed my mind. "Hell, he's the one who gave me my nipple rings on our second anniversary together. Mike had rings in both of his nipples, and he thought that I needed my tits pierced, as well. We had a really hot scene that night, with a friend of Mike's who ran a tattoo and piercing shop in town. I remember that the two of them spread me out on the cross, and gave me a really intense session of chest and nipple flogging and tortures that lasted for over two hours, that ended with Mike's friend piercing my tits and putting in the rings while I was spread-eagled, without anything to kill the pain. I never screamed as long or as loud as that night!"

Wolf shivered a little at that and said; "Whoa, I really would have loved to have been there that night, Sir."

"Why? I thought you only liked being tortured yourself, boy, not watching someone else get worked over."

He smirked at me and slyly said; "Maybe they would have wanted a second victim, Sir!"

I rolled my eyes and sighed; "Jeez, Chuck was right! You are a horny one, boy! All right, boy, when you're all healed up, I guess we'll have to see just how much your tits can really take, and maybe if you're really good, you might get a set of rings in those big nipples of yours!"

Wolf just leaned back against my chest and softly moaned; "When I'm healed, I'll take you up on that offer, Sir!"

I gave him a light hug, and continued; "Mike did a good job of training me, but first he had to break me of all the old habits I had developed and then had to start from scratch on teaching me the right way to be a top and a master. It was a slow process at first, since I was still pretty bull-headed at the time, you know, all full of piss and vinegar, and had to be re-educated. We had some epic battles at first, but since Mike was stronger and much better trained in police techniques for subduing unruly individuals, he always won. And unfortunately for me, losing one of our fights invariably ended up with me enduring some pretty strict discipline and painful torture. So when I told you once that I've never done anything to you with the exception of one, or two things now I guess, that I haven't had done to me, I wasn't kidding! I've been stretched on the rack, staked out in the backyard, hung by my arms and been flogged, spent many nights chained up in the cell, and almost anything else that could be done to someone in the dungeon. Mike always knew how to take me right to the edge of my endurance, without pushing me over the brink. He told me that being able to take a slave to the edge, and then keeping him there for several hours was also a part of being a good topman."

"Knowing how strong and vital he had been made it even harder the last few weeks that Mike was alive. He had asked all his friends to stop coming over to see him, as he didn't want them to see him as sick as he was. I guess the hardest day that I had to endure since the death of my parents was the day that Mike finally died."

"He knew that the end was coming, and even though the doctors wanted him in the hospital, we both agreed that he wanted to go at home. He spent a couple of hours sitting up in his big lounge chair in the bay window in the master bedroom that overlooked San Francisco Bay. Finally, he asked me to put him to bed. I could pick him up and carry him easily by then, as he was so thin."

"I put him in his bed, put on his favorite music, which was some Mozart, and then he asked me to just hold him, since for the first time in his life, he was afraid! I crawled into bed with him and wrapped my arms around his painfully thin frame, and just held on, rocking him gently as I listened to his breath rattling in his throat."

"We lay there together for at least a half hour. I knew deep in my heart that this was the last time I would ever get to hold the man who had meant so much to me, and had saved my life!"

"Then, at last, he opened his eyes and looked at me. 'I'm going to be leaving you now, boy. You remember all the things I've taught you. I want you to be the best master in the city!'"

"I looked into his eyes and promised; 'Yes Sir, I will, Sir. I love you, Master Michael!'"

"He just closed his eyes and, gently smiling, softly murmured; 'Good boy! I love you too, Master Eric.'"

"I started to cry then, as this was the first time he had ever called me that. I knew it was his way of saying that my training was over and I was ready to continue on my own. I just held him for about another five minutes until his breathing slowed and then, taking one last breath, he just stopped breathing, and I knew his long fight was over. At least, I knew he had gone the way he wanted, peacefully at home and in his own bed."

Wolf sat there silently for a while with tears streaming down his cheeks. Hell, I was crying at the memories, as well! Finally, he turned to me and without saying a word began to kiss away the tears that were running down my face. After a few moments he whispered; "I'm so sorry, Sir."

His kisses became more intense, until we were deep kissing and tonguing each other. Wolf then slowly began to work his way down my neck and along my jaw, nuzzling and kissing me. He slowly opened up my robe, and began to work his way down my chest. He finally worked his way down to where he could suck on my nipples gently, first one then the other. I just sighed with pleasure and let him work on my chest for a while. Finally, he pulled back and then knelt in front of me, spreading my robe completely open.

Wolf bent down and began to gently chew on my fully erect cock through the thin cotton gym shorts I wore under my robe. I moaned with pleasure as the wonderful sensations of warmth began to spread through my cock and balls from Wolf's hot mouth. Eventually, he slipped my throbbing cock out of the waistband of the shorts. His mouth surrounded my erect shaft, as he slowly worked the shorts down and off my legs. I just leaned back and relaxed as Wolf's head bobbed up and down as he gave me one of his always-great blowjobs. His strong hands stroked up and down my torso, caressing each muscle as he worshipped my dick with his mouth. Shortly, I reached down and held on to his head, caressing and stroking his long hair, as I began to thrust into his hot, sucking mouth faster and faster until, with a gasp of pleasure, I shot a thick hot load deeply into his mouth. Wolf moaned as my sperm filled his mouth. I could feel his tongue on my dickhead as he sucked every last drop of my load into his mouth and swallowed it.

Finally, Wolf leaned back on his knees and, licking his lips, said; "Thank you, Sir. I hope that helped you feel a little better!"

I smiled down at him and said; "Boy, you always make me feel better! I guess telling someone about Mike just brought back some feelings that I haven't had to deal with for a while."

Wolf looked a little concerned as he asked me; "Sir, I hope you don't think what I just did was inappropriate, do you? I just wanted to help. I didn't want to lessen your memories, or try to compete with them in any way!"

I smiled down at him and then told him to sit back on the couch between my legs. He settled back, his hard muscled back pressed against my bare chest as I wrapped my arms around him, being careful to avoid putting my hands on his tits under his t-shirt, and softly told him; "Don't worry about that, boy. My memories of Mike are good, and I loved him, and always will, but it's the kind of love a slave has for his master. It's a different feeling than I have for you. I think I love you more completely that I ever did Mike. It's hard to explain, and I've never tried to compare the two feelings before."

I chuckled lightly and added, "Besides, I didn't tell you to stop, did I? Don't worry about it. I think if Mike were here, he would have approved. Hell, he probably would have had you suck him off next!"

Wolf turned and grinned as he said; "Thank you, Sir. I would have been honored, and I really think I know about the love a slave can have for his master!"

We just sat silently for a while, listening to the rain as it continued to fall in sheets and occasionally blew against the windows of the living room, with me holding on to Wolf's hard body, just enjoying the warmth of him, the clean scent of his hair, and reflecting on the closeness we shared as both lovers and as master and slave. We stayed like that for a while, both of us thinking our own thoughts until Wolf leaned his head back and rested it on my shoulder.

It looked like he was on the verge of falling asleep, so I whispered into his ear; "Come on boy, I think it's time for bed. It's been a long day, and a long week for both of us."

Wolf just murmured his assent. We both got up and made our way upstairs.

I asked him; "Do you want to sleep with me, or do you want to sleep in your own bed, boy?

He sleepily looked at me and yawned before answering; "I'm so pooped right now, Sir, that I don't think it would make a lot of difference."

I smiled at him and said; "All right then, boy. Into your own bed tonight.

You need a good nights sleep."

I took him into his room and gently tucked my tired, battered, still slightly sun burnt slave boy into bed. "You sleep good tonight, boy. You need to start healing, so I can torture you some more, and maybe even give you a set of nipple rings, if you're good, slave."

He blearily looked up and mumbled; "Yes, Sir! I'm looking forward to it, Sir!"

I leaned down to kiss him goodnight and then stood to go to my own room. I think Wolf was fast asleep by the time I got to the door of his room. I stopped at the door, turned and smiled at my now sleeping lover. As I turned off the light and closed the door, I softly whispered; "Good night my love. Sleep well."

Chapter Thirteen
Eddie's Punishment

Over the next couple of weeks, we had to change our regular routine as Wolf's nipples healed from their branding, and as he recovered from the almost unbearable tortures I had subjected him to at the ranch. It seemed that he had endured the suffering with almost no long-term effects. He was sore for a week or so from a minor strain of one of his shoulders from the torture by the horses, and I took him to a dermatologist friend of mine to check on his tits, but all in all, he came through the ordeal in good shape.

Danny, my best friend in town, and his boy Eddie Wong, a slim but wiry hard muscled and tattooed 25-year-old Chinese-American boy, met us one Friday night in the Eagle about three weeks after we returned from our trip. Danny and I had done several scenes with both boys, as Eddie had almost a high pain tolerance as Wolf, although he wasn't nearly as strong. I also knew that Eddie was really hot for Wolf. Only once before, on Eddie's last birthday, had Danny and I agreed to give him a treat, and let him and Wolf have a session of hot, sweaty man sex together, while Danny and I watched. Eddie was one of the few people, along with Danny, that I would let cum in Wolf's mouth or ass. I knew they were both safe for bareback sex, since Danny was very vigilant about their health.

They both were surprised, as was everyone else who knew us at the Eagle, when I led Wolf in on the end of his leash wearing his new chaps as well as a shirt covering his nipple bandages. I rarely allowed Wolf to wear a shirt at the bar, unless it was cold enough to require it. I thought that Eddie was going to have an orgasm right there in the bar when I had Wolf take off his shirt and show them his new brandings!

We sat at one of the tables in the bar with Wolf and Eddie kneeling beside our chairs, where Wolf and I told them the story of what we had done at the ranch. By the time we were done with our story, Eddie was practically pleading with Danny to go to the ranch sometime to see if he could endure some of the same tortures as Wolf.

He actually started to get pushy about it, loudly insisting that Danny needed to plan a trip to the ranch as soon as possible. Danny stood up, and grabbing his collar, pulled Eddie to his feet, snarling; "What the fuck do you think you're doing, boy? How dare you whine and snivel in front of my friends and especially in front of Master Eric! And then you think you can tell me what I need to do about going to the ranch? You're gonna regret that, punk!"

Eddie immediately cowered in front of his enraged master, and whispered; "Oh God, I'm sorry, Sir! Please forgive me, Master!" He then knelt down and began to lick Danny's boots in supplication. Danny pushed him back, and growled; "That's not gonna help, punk. You just earned yourself some major punishment! I think both Master Eric and I need to beat some respect and obedience back into you!"

Danny turned to me and said; "What do you think we ought to do with this worthless piece of shit, Master Eric?" Eddie moaned softly when he heard his master refer to me by my full title. The few times that he had ever heard that before, it had cost him days of recovery from the tortures Danny and I had subjected him to.

Wolf, on the other hand, remained perfectly still; kneeling next to the chair I was sitting in and knowing that the slightest bit of incorrect behavior on his part would result in his being subjected to the same tortures that Eddie was going to face, half-healed nipples notwithstanding! I think that he knew that my temper had been tripped by Eddie's insolent behavior towards his master.

I stood up and stared coldly down at the trembling slave groveling on the cold concrete floor of the bar. Several other masters and slaves were watching the unfolding drama taking place at our table. I reached out with my foot, and looking at Danny and getting a slight nod of his head, I pushed Eddie onto his side on the floor, and then kept rolling him over until he was lying on his back. I then put my right foot across his throat on top of his collar, and started to put just the slightest pressure on his throat. Eddie went stock-still, barely daring to breathe! He stared up at the ceiling, his eyes wide with fear.

"I think he needs some remedial training in what it means to be a slave, Master Daniel!"

Eddie moaned again at the sound of his master's full name. He knew he was in trouble with the both of us!

I looked at Danny and asked; "Your dungeon, or mine?" Danny's was closer, but mine was better equipped. Danny thought for a second and then said; "Well, I don't have to be anywhere soon, so why don't we use yours, Master Eric."

I nodded and then, removing my foot from Eddie's throat, told Wolf;

"Stand up, boy."

Wolf immediately shot to his feet, and then stood silently with his hands crossed behind his back and his eyes down, while Danny told Eddie to stand. Danny then snapped a pair of handcuffs on Eddie and led him out of the bar by the leash attached to the d-ring on his collar, followed by Wolf and I.

On the drive back home, with Danny and Eddie following in their car, I was silent while I planned tonight's scenes. Wolf knew not to say anything that could get me mad at him in my current state of mind.

When we arrived at my house, I gave Wolf a list of chores to attend to while Danny was preparing Eddie for his punishment. Eddie was stripped down to his boots and collar, and then spread-eagled in chains under one of the ceiling beams of the dungeon, his feet spread wide and fastened to eye bolts in the floor. Danny then told his slave to open his mouth as wide as he could, and when Eddie did; Danny stuffed a ball gag in, and strapped it around Eddie's head. Danny then stepped back and waited for me while I went upstairs to change. When he saw me, Eddie moaned softly into his gag. I had changed from the clothes I was wearing at the bar into just a pair of chaps, my tall biker boots, a jock pouch and my mirrored shades. Eddie and Wolf both knew when I dressed like that for a dungeon scene, I was serious!

I stood in front of the helpless slave, and asked his master; "How badly are you planning on hurting him tonight?"

Danny glared at Eddie while he removed his shirt and told me; "He's going right to the edge tonight, and he's gonna stay there for as long as I think it will take for this worthless piece of shit to learn some respect and manners!"

Eddie just whimpered. Danny stepped up and laid two hard slaps across Eddie's face at the sound! "What the fuck do you think you're doing, boy?" he screamed in Eddie's ear.

"Who the hell told you that you could make a sound, slave?"

Eddie just hung his head, tears starting to stream down his cheeks. About this time, Wolf walked back into the dungeon and merely nodded his head, signifying that he had finished the tasks I had sent him to do. He knelt silently next to the master's seat that was in one corner of the main room of the dungeon, and waited for me.

I walked over to the seat and sat down to watch what Danny was going to do to punish his errant slave boy. Eddie could only stand helplessly and wait for whatever torture he was going to have to endure.

Danny started by picking up one of my medium weight floggers and started to work it across Eddie's torso, starting on his back and working around to Eddie's chest and abs, striping the skin, and then slowly turning it redder and redder with each stroke of the cat.

Eddie could do nothing but twist and writhe as the blows started getting harder and harder as Danny slowly ramped up the intensity of the flogging. The sweat was beginning to shine on both Danny's and Eddie's bodies from the exertion of the flogging, and the warmth of the dungeon.

Danny then said, "Master Eric, do you want to help me work on this worthless thing?"

I nodded and walked over and picked up my favorite heavyweight cat from the toy rack, and began to work on Eddie's chest, while Danny went back to working on his back.

Eddie started shrieking into the gag filling his mouth as two separate floggers lashed his already striped skin at the same time!

After a full fifteen minutes of whipping his slave, Danny announced; "Now that he's fully aware of what's gonna happen to him tonight, I think it's time we started to torture this piece of shit, don't you, Master Eric?"

I slowly walked over to the helpless slave, hanging in his chains and gasping for air. I grabbed his throat and forced him to look directly into my eyes.

I saw a look of real fear in his face as I growled; "Whatever you want to do to it is all right with me, Master Daniel. The only thing I ask is that you get rid of the body if you need to!"

Eddie's eyes went even wider with fear, and I saw a look of real panic begin to creep into his eyes. I think he was actually afraid for his safety for just a few minutes! Eddie hadn't been a slave long enough to know that a good master would not consciously cause any real long-term damage to his slave. What Danny and I were doing to him was all part of the psychological aspects of a heavy S+M scene. His chest began to heave faster and faster as Eddie started to hyperventilate with real fear! Finally, he just broke down and started to cry, the tears flowing down his cheeks as he sobbed into the gag filling his mouth.

Danny pulled over the small table from its space in the corner of the dungeon and started to set up the equipment that we were going to use to torture Eddie. He could only watch helplessly, his eyes widening as each piece of torture equipment was set out in front of him. Danny had brought his own equipment box with him and he pulled his electrical equipment from it. There was a small TENS unit for electrical stimulation of select body parts, and a larger version of an older relaxicisor unit, which did the same thing, but could be attached to more body parts at the same time.

Danny attached a pair of small plastic clamps with leads running to imbedded electrical contacts to the TENS box and set the clamps on Eddie's nipples. The clamps would send an electric impulse through the nipple without the current flowing across Eddie's chest, which could be potentially damaging or even lethal. Electricity near the heart always had to be done carefully.

Next, Danny knelt down and wrapped lengths of leather thongs around each of Eddie's balls, separating them. Then a thin stripped wire was wrapped around each ball several times and the bare ends of the wires were clipped to leads plugged into the larger electrical box. Other leads were fastened to hose clamps fastened around Eddie's throbbing cock, one at the base, and one just under the head. Another lead was attached to a clear Lucite butt plug with imbedded contact points on the surface.

Eddie moaned and strained against his bonds as the plug was lubed and slowly pushed up his ass until the entire eight inches were imbedded inside his body. Finally, Danny took a long, thin tube of what looked like rubber encased with a thin coating of metal and, after lubing it thoroughly, began to slide it up inside the head of Eddie's cock. Eddie moaned and writhed as he felt the tube slipping deeper and deeper inside his Urethra until the tube was pushed in the entire seven inches of his cock. You could actually see the skin of his cock stretch and bulge as the tube slid inside of it.

Danny then attached leads from the electrical box to all the torture devices attached to his slave's genitals. Eddie could only stare down, an expression of fear mixed with anticipation in his eyes as his master prepared to torture him. I told Wolf to take the power cord from the box and plug it into the wall outlet. The TENS unit was battery powered and had no cord.

Danny stood up in front of his helpless, bound boy and flipped on the switch of the larger electrical box. A low, menacing hum emanated from the box. Eddie's breathing became more and more rapid, as he began to anticipate the pain and suffering he was about to endure. Danny handed me the TENS unit and said; "Master Eric, you can have his nipples!"

I keyed the switch on the box and turned the first control knob to send the first slight jolt of power through Eddie's nipples. He stiffened as the current zapped through his tits for just a second or so, his muscles flexing under his skin. Eddie couldn't have had more then three or four percent body fat. As a matter of fact, he looked like an anatomical chart showing the muscles of a man's body, only with a coating of very thin skin over the muscles. He wasn't bulky at all, but worked out constantly and was the single most ripped man I had ever seen in my life.

His body stiffened again and then began to twitch as Danny started to send electrical impulses through Eddie's cock, balls, and ass! The unit was set up so any two contacts would work as a positive and a negative, so the current could flow from Eddie's cockhead to his asshole, his left nut to the shaft inside his dick, and so forth. The box could also be set to send random impulses to any combination of leads, in a randomly variable order and levels of intensity and duration.

Eddie began to writhe and moan into his gag as Danny slowly turned up the power flowing into Eddie's body. I slowly increased the input to his nipples at the same time. Eddie's muscles began to flex harder and harder as the power increased, the tendons and veins starting to pop out on his arms and across his chest and shoulders. The sweat was running down his twitching body, as Danny and I increased his level of suffering slowly and teasingly. I knew from personal experience with Mike that Eddie's nipples felt like they were being pierced with red-hot needles, while his cock and balls felt like they were being dipped in boiling water and then encased in ice, as the electrical currents overloaded the pain receptors in his genitals.

Every time an impulse of electricity hit the plug in Eddie's ass, the sphincter muscle would contract automatically, forcing the plug in further. If set up properly, a slave could be forced to fuck himself with the plug, and there wasn't a thing he could do about it! Also, when an impulse hit his cock, either in one of the hose clamps or in the imbedded tube, Eddie's cock would swell up and twitch.

We tortured Danny's slave for a good fifteen minutes, slowly increasing the power of the current slamming into his nipples and genitals. Eddie was desperately writhing and twisting in his chains, but there wasn't anything he could do but endure the punishment torture he was being subjected to. He was screaming and howling into his gag, but to no avail. He had earned this torture with his behavior, and he had no choice but to suffer!

I had an idea of how to increase the suffering Eddie had to endure, so I set the TENS unit to deliver random jolts of power to Eddie's nipples for variable levels of intensity and duration. I set the TENS unit box on the table next to Eddie's writhing, twisting body and told Wolf to go and get my UV wand from the shelf where I kept it. During the entire time of Eddie's torture, Wolf had stayed in his position kneeling next to my chair, except when I told him to perform a specific task. I knew he was desperately wanting to participate in Eddie's torture, but he hadn't broken discipline! I was proud of him for that.

When he brought my UV wand to me, I told Wolf to kneel in front of Eddie and watch him suffer, and told him loudly, so Eddie could hear; "See boy, this is what happens when you are a disobedient piece of shit that wants to think he's a slave, but is nothing but a pretender. But when we're done with him, he'll either be a proper slave, or he'll be running home to mommy, crying all the way!"

Danny turned and looked at me, a quizzical expression on his face until I winked at him. His mouth quirked up in a smile, which he then forced off his face before he turned back to torturing his boy.

I opened up the UV wand's box and set up the unit with the rake attachment on it. It looked like a small five tined garden rake made of glass tubing plugged into the power unit. I turned on the power and increased the setting until the neon gas inside the rake began to glow, and the unit made a vaguely threatening humming sound.

I stepped behind Eddie's body and began to run the rake down his hard muscled, writhing back. From each of the tines of the rake, a fat spark of static electricity arced to Eddie's glistening skin! He threw his head back and shrieked into his gag at this new source of torment. I worked the rake over the entire surface of his back and shoulders, loving the look of the hard muscles flexing and rippling under his tattooed skin. Eddie had a tattoo of a Chinese dragon on his left pec, intricate characters on both of his thick delts and shoulders, and a spread winged phoenix across the width of his upper back.

I slowly worked the rake down to his lower back, where he had a classic pattern of muscle rippling under his skin that bodybuilders called a Christmas tree. Eddie howled harder when I started to run the rake over the hard globes of his ass. His muscles worked harder and harder the longer I tortured him with the wand. Danny was increasing the intensity of the current flowing into Eddie the entire time I was doing his back. Eddie was almost in a frenzy by now, desperately struggling but totally unable to escape the agony tearing through him!

I moved in front of Eddie, and changed the attachment on the UV wand to a single tube with an enlarged, mushroom shaped head. I turned the wand back on, this tine setting the power on full. Eddie stared down at the wand with total fear in his eyes when I slowly brought the mushroom in towards his left armpit. Danny kept Eddie's pits and crotch shaved smooth, so there was no hair to get in the way of the electrical arc. Eddie shrieked again into the gag when the thick spark leapt from the wand to the skin of his pit.

I tortured both of his pits, and then worked the mushroom across Eddie's pecs, down over his heaving, rippling ribcage, over the muscles straining on his sides, and then across his flat, ripped abdominal muscles. Eddie was only about the second or third person I had ever seen in my life who actually had an eight pack of ab muscles. His abs were flexing and knotting every time a jolt of electricity shot into one or both of his nipples, or through his cock and balls and his asshole! The tears were running freely down his face as he cried and howled into his gag constantly.

Wolf was still kneeling where I had left him, but he was now watching Eddie endure his torture. Wolf's cock was fully hard as he knelt, but he kept his hands crossed tightly across his lower back, since I had not given him permission to touch himself.

The torture continued about another five minutes, until Danny bent down in front of Eddie and slowly withdrew the tube of metal lined rubber from his cock. Eddie strained at the feel of the tube being pulled out of his dickhead. Danny announced; "It's time to see what he can take! Master Eric, may I use slave Wolf to help?"

I told him; "Certainly, Master Daniel. He's yours to command!"

Danny told Wolf to lean in and keep his mouth close to the head of Eddie's cock. Danny turned to me and said; "No need letting him make a mess on the floor when there's a perfectly good mouth available!"

I grinned, but then stood back to watch what was going to happen. Danny slowly started to turn the levels of power up higher and higher, until Eddie was shrieking constantly into his gag. Danny then leaned in and unbuckled the gag from around Eddie's head and pulled it out of his mouth. He snarled at his slave; "I want to hear you scream in agony, punk! Scream for me, shitboy!"

At that, Danny turned the power on all the knobs of the control box up full! Eddie threw his head back and shrieked "AAAUUUGHHHHH!!!" as loud as I had ever heard anyone scream in my dungeon. Every muscle on his body flexed to the utmost, quivering and shaking. His feet actually started to lift off of the floor, as his biceps and pecs knotted and bulged. The cords were standing out on his neck and across his rippling, bulging shoulders.

Finally with one last scream of "OOOH FUUUUUCCCK, MAAAASTER!!" Eddie shot a thick hard jet of cum directly into Wolf's waiting mouth. The streams of sperm continued to shoot out as Danny kept the current flowing through Eddie's nuts and cock. Eddie shrieked again and again as his nuts were forced to drain themselves into Wolf's mouth. Finally, Eddie slumped down, hanging limp in the chains, his eyes closed and his tortured orgasm spent!

Danny ordered Wolf to back out of the way before cutting off the power to the electrical box torturing Eddie. I stepped in and helped him remove the clamps and wires attached to his helpless slave's limp body. Eddie was moaning softly, his chest rising and falling rapidly as he tried to recover from having a huge load tortured out of him. Danny lifted Eddie's head and checked his slave to be sure that he was all right. We both knew that Danny would not risk injuring Eddie, but he still needed to discipline him.

I told Wolf to stand up and hold Eddie while Danny and I released him from his bonds. Wolf wrapped his arms around him and hugged Eddie tightly to hold him up. When he was released, I told Wolf to help him to the cot in the corner. Wolf had to almost carry Eddie there, as he had almost no control over his own muscles yet. They were almost the same height, but Wolf was a good thirty pounds heavier, and it was all muscle.

When he was on the cot, Danny checked up more fully on his slave, while I told Wolf to kneel in front of me. I was so turned on by the sight of Eddie's hot physique being forced to endure almost unbearable levels of torture that I almost couldn't stand it. I unsnapped my jock pouch and immediately forced my fully hard cock into Wolf's waiting mouth. I reached down and held tightly to his head, and started to rape Wolf's hot, sucking mouth harder and harder. His hands wrapped around my legs for support while I ravaged him.

Within seconds, I threw my head back and growled; "Oh yeah, take it, slave. Swallow your master's cum! Take it!" while I shot a huge load deeply into Wolf's mouth. The muscles in his throat worked as he swallowed my sperm. I stood there for a few seconds, panting and gasping for air until I pulled my cock out of Wolf's mouth. He looked up at me and seemed ready to say something until I signaled him for silence. I turned to where Danny was tending to his tortured slave. Eddie seemed to be coming around, so I told Wolf to go get a cup of water from the bathroom in the dungeon and give it to Eddie. Eddie managed to sit up by the time Wolf returned. He accepted the water gratefully, and when he was done drinking, slipped off of the cot and knelt in front of his master, his hands crossed behind his back, and his head down. He started to cry as he knelt there. Danny lifted Eddie's face up and looked into his eyes.

"Do you think you've learned your lesson, punk, or do you need more reminding what being a slave is all about?" Danny asked him coldly.

Eddie moaned and replied; "That's not my call to make, Sir. Only you can decide that, Sir. My fate is totally yours to decide, Master!"

Dally growled; "Good answer, punk, but I think you still need another reminder!" Eddie merely moaned. Danny turned to me and asked; "Master Eric, what do you think he needs next?"

I smiled evilly down at the kneeling, trembling slave at our feet and said; "I have just the perfect torture for this punk boy. Stand up and follow me, slave."

Eddie rose to his feet shakily and followed me as I led him into the room of the dungeon that led to the door outside to the pool area in the back yard. He moaned when he figured out what I was going to do to him. Danny stepped in and gave Eddie two quick slaps across the face and snarled; "Shut up, punk. You earned this so don't complain!"

I led Eddie into the sauna that was in the corner of the room next to the outside door and told him to stand in the middle of the stifling hot room. One of the tasks I had told Wolf to do when we got home from the bar was to turn on the sauna full. Within minutes I had Eddie standing spread-eagled in the sauna, his wrists and ankles fastened to restraints in the overhead beam and base of the bench built into the sauna. I looked at the thermometer on the wall, and saw that it was nearing 190 degrees. The sauna would go to over 225 if left on long enough.

Next, to add to his agony, I clipped the excruciatingly painful alligator nipple clamps to Eddie's already tender tits. He howled and screamed in agony, his lean body writhing in pain as the each clamp was attached to each of his tits, biting deeply into the thick nubs of flesh.

When he was secured, I turned to Danny and Wolf, who stood there watching me secure the helpless slave for his next torture and told them; "Let's let him cook for a couple of hours with those clamps on and see if that helps change his attitude!"

Danny merely smiled and said; "That's why I like you Master Eric. You're an evil bastard!"

We both laughed cruelly as we turned to leave. I told Wolf; "Upstairs, boy. I think Master Daniel needs someone to fuck, and I know that I do. You're elected!"

As we left, I turned back to Eddie, stretched helplessly to roast in the middle of the blazing hot room and said; "Just to remind you of what you can't have until your master says so, here!" He moaned when I set a full can of soda from the small fridge in the corner in the window of the sauna, where he could see it, but that was all.

The sweat was already pouring down his lean, hard body and dripping on the floor, and his breath was already rasping in his throat when I closed the door, leaving Eddie alone to cook in the sauna in near darkness. Only the dim red light in the corner of the sauna gave him any illumination. The last thing I heard before the door closed was the sound of the tortured boy starting to softly cry as though his heart was breaking, and his soul had been totally ripped away.

Chapter Fourteen
Dues

Wolf, Danny and I went upstairs to the master bedroom where I ordered Wolf to undress me, hang my leathers up to air out, and then do the same for Danny. I kept an eye on the clock to make sure that Eddie didn't get left alone in the intense heat of the sauna for too long a time. We wanted him to suffer, but not for him to risk any injury. I figured about thirty minutes cooking in the heat would be enough, contrary to the several hours I had told Eddie. I had told him that just to mess with his head. Mental torture can be almost as effective as physical torture.

I told Wolf to kneel on the floor between us and suck my cock. He went to work with his hot mouth for a few minutes, while Danny stepped behind me, wrapped his arms around me, and played with my nipples and my rings. I had Wolf suck me for just a few minutes before I took my cock out of his mouth and asked Danny if he wanted to fuck Wolf, or get sucked off by him, or what he wanted to do to my slave.

He grinned at me and said; "I think I really want to try out that hot ass of his, since I haven't had it for a while. I bet with all the bodybuilding you guys have done, that ass is gonna be nice and tight, and those butt muscles are gonna really be hard!"

I chuckled but then got serious as I told Wolf; "Boy, you are to serve Master Daniel just like you would serve me. Anything he wants you to do, you are to do. If he wants to cum in your mouth, you are to take his load. If he wants to cum in your ass, you will let him. I know that he is safe, and you will obey him. Is that clear, slave?"

Wolf looked up at me from his kneeling position and softly said; "Yes, Master. I will serve Master Daniel however he wants me to. I will take his load if he thinks I am worthy of it."

I stroked his hair and told him; "Good boy. I need to go down and check on the punk boy cooking in the dungeon. You two have fun, but I have one more order. Wolf, don't cum! I want you to save your load for that punk boy.

He's gonna be forced to take a slave's load in his mouth or ass, wherever we tell you to give it to him. Is that understood, boy?"

Wolf nodded. "Yes Sir, I won't cum, Sir."

I looked at Danny and said; "Use him however you want and have fun!"

I went downstairs and waited for the proper time to go down into the dungeon, naked except for my boots to observe how Eddie was enduring his roasting in the sauna.

When I finally went downstairs into the torture chamber, I stopped and got a couple of bottles of water out of the fridge in the corner, and stepped in front of the window of the sauna that looked out into the dungeon. Eddie hung limply in his restraints, his entire weight being supported by his wide-spread arms, as his knees had buckled, with his head down with his chin resting on his chest. His chest rose and fell erratically as he gasped for air in the intense heat of the sauna. Every rib and muscle in his torso stood out and rippled with his every movement. His entire body was glistening and dripping wet with sweat in the dim red light, and there was actually a wet spot on the floor where the sweat dripped off of his body and onto the floor faster than it could be evaporated in the heat.

Eddie lifted his head when he heard me open the door, and weakly moaned; "Master Eric, help me please. I can't take any more. Please Sir, whatever you want me to do, I'll do it. Please, help me, Sir. I just can't take any more! I'm at the end of my strength, Sir!"

His head dropped back down on his chest as he began to cry, deep racking sobs that seemed to come from his very core. I could tell that he wasn't acting, or putting on a show for me, but that he was on the very edge of totally and completely breaking down.

I stepped up to him and lifted up his head with a hand under his chin. I held one of the bottles of water up to his quivering lips and told him; "Take a sip, boy. Just a sip!"

Eddie swallowed a bit of the water and then coughed and gasped as the cold water coursed down his parched throat. I waited a second or two and then gave him some more water. It took about two or three minutes for him to drink the whole bottle, but when he was done, he seemed to be a bit stronger. Eddie gathered himself together and got his feet under himself and stood back up, relieving some of the pressure on his arms.

"Thank you, Sir. I'm sorry, Sir. I'm so very sorry, Sir!" he softly moaned.

I stepped back, crossed my arms across my chest, and just looked into his eyes, glowering at him, until he dropped his head.

"I'm not the one you need to apologize to, boy!" I growled at him. "The person you need to apologize to is your master. You were extremely disrespectful to him, especially in public, and now you're paying the price for that disrespect, boy!"

Eddie started to cry again and then sobbed; "Oh God, I'm so sorry! I love Master Daniel, and I wouldn't ever want to do anything to disappoint him. How can I make it up to him, Master Eric? Please, Sir, help me. Tell me what to do, Sir!"

"Don't ask me, boy. I have no idea what your master wants to do to you next, boy. He might be finished punishing you, or he may just be starting!"

Eddie just moaned. I stepped up to him and lifted his sweat and tear-streaked face up so I could look into his red-rimmed eyes.

"I'll give you one little bit of advice. If I were you, I would grovel like never before, slave. Now, stand up straight and keep your balance and I'll get you out of here."

Eddie pulled himself back upright. I stepped in front of him and reached out to the clamps on Eddie's nipples. I heard him groan in anticipation of the pain that was about to hit his entire body. When I did squeeze the clamps to remove them, Eddie threw his head back and screamed at the sudden rush of agony. Every muscle in his wiry torso flexed to its limit as I then rolled his nipples between my fingers to restore the circulation.

Eddie was gasping for air and retching by the time I finished working on his tortured tits. I knelt down and unfastened the restraints from the bottom of the bench, allowing him to put his feet together. I stood up and undid the restraint on his right wrist from the eyehook it was clipped to. I gently lowered his arm down to his side, and then repeated the procedure for his other arm. He moaned again as he wrapped his arms around my shoulders for support as I lowered him down to a sitting position on the bench. We sat for just a few moments until I told Eddie; "Let's get out of here, boy. It's too hot to sit any longer."

As soon as we walked into the dungeon, Eddie started to shiver in the relative coolness of the room. It was hot compared to the rest of the house, but considerably cooler then the sauna. I led him to the shower in the small bathroom, removed the restraints from his wrists and ankles and told him to take a warm shower to cool himself down slowly, and then wait in the dungeon until someone came down to get him. He assured me that he would await the return of either me or Danny and then knelt in front of me and kissed my boots.

While Eddie showered, I went back upstairs to see how Danny and Wolf were getting along.

When I walked into the bedroom, Wolf was squatting across Danny on the floor of the bedroom, facing away from Danny, with Danny's hard cock impaling Wolf's tight ass. The sweat was streaking down Wolf's chest and back as Danny thrust his hips up and down under Wolf, driving his cock in and out of Wolf's hole. I watched for a few minutes, before I stepped in front of Wolf and said; "Open up, boy!"

Wolf opened his mouth wide as I thrust my rapidly enlarging cock into that hot hole. Wolf moaned around my cock at the feel of having over sixteen inches of man cock pushed into his body from two directions at the same time!

Danny increased the speed of his thrusting, the muscles in his hard torso flexing and contracting as he fucked my slave's tight hole.

In just another minute or two, Danny groaned; "Oh fuck, I'm gonna cum! Ride that cock, boy! Shit, yeah!"

He then threw back his head and yelled; "Oh yeah!" as he pumped his load deeply into Wolf's ass. Wolf moaned around my cock again at the feel of the hot sperm hosing into his hole.

When Danny's orgasm was finally spent and he lay back on the floor, his chest heaving, I pulled my cock out of Wolf's mouth and told them both; "That looked like fun!"

Both of them grinned at me. Danny panted; "Trust me, Eric, it was!"

I told them about telling Eddie to await our return to the dungeon to see what other punishment he would have to endure. I also told Danny that I thought that Eddie had learned his lesson, but that it was Danny's call to decide if Eddie needed any more working over.

Danny smiled wolfishly and said; "There's only a couple more things for him to endure before I'll call it a night for him."

Danny turned to Wolf and told him; "I want you to fuck that boy of mine. It's a real humiliation for a slave to be fucked by another slave. He'll get that little lesson in humility first, but then he's gonna get one more that will last a while."

We walked downstairs into the dungeon to find Eddie kneeling in the middle of the floor, his head down, crying softly to himself with his hands crossed behind his back.

Danny stepped in front of his slave and snarled; "Well boy, have you learned your lesson yet?"

Eddie softly said; "Oh Master, I'm so sorry for what I did, Sir. It was unforgivable, Sir.

Please accept my apologies for my behavior. I embarrassed you in front of your friends, and I'm so sorry, Sir!"

By now, the tears were streaking down his face again, and his body was being racked with sobs. Danny stared coldly down at his groveling, miserable slave, and just stood there. I knew Danny well enough to know that he wasn't really that cold hearted of a bastard, but he was putting on an act for his boy's benefit. Finally he told Eddie: "O.K. boy, endure two more things tonight, and then I might think about starting to consider forgiving you eventually!"

Eddie looked up and said; "Yes, Sir. Whatever you want to do to me, Master. I've earned any more punishments you wish to inflict on me, Sir!"

Danny turned to me and asked; "Do you have the restraints handy? We'll need them."

I sent Wolf to get them from the other room near the shower. When he had returned, Danny led Eddie over to the sling in a corner of the dungeon. "In, boy" was all he said.

Eddie climbed into the sling, and within minutes was totally restrained in a stretched spread-eagle position, his legs spread wide exposing his ass, and his arms stretched along the chains supporting the head end of the sling.

Danny then turned to Wolf and ordered him; "All right, slave. I want you to humiliate this worthless fuckup one more time, and fuck him. Fuck him hard and deep, and make him take your slave cum either in his ass or in his mouth!"

Eddie moaned softly because he knew that for a slave to be essentially raped by another slave was a true humiliation. It meant that in his master's eyes, he was lower than low.

Wolf stepped between Eddie's spread legs and stroked his thick cock until it was fully hard. He spread some lube on his shaft, positioned himself, and then with a single powerful thrust of his muscled torso, drove the entire length of the fat shaft deeply into Eddie's hot tight hole! Eddie threw back his head and screamed as he felt the cock slam into his body. Danny and I both knew that Eddie loved taking Wolf's cock in his ass, but not like this!

Wolf grasped Eddie's hips and began thrusting himself back and forth, growling and grunting as the thick length of his engorged cock drove in and out of Eddie's ravaged hole.

Wolf fucked the helpless slave for a good ten minutes, Eddie howling and moaning the entire time, until Wolf gasped; "I'm gonna cum, Sir! Do you want me to shoot in his ass or his mouth, Sir?"

Danny ordered Wolf; "Put that cock in his mouth, slave. Let him clean it with his mouth while you fuck his face!"

Wolf stepped back and quickly walked around to where he could drive his cock into Eddie's sucking mouth. He grasped Eddie's head and bent it down backwards, stretching his neck as he started pumping his cock in and out. Within thirty seconds Wolf gasped; "Oh shit, I'm cumming, Sir!" He threw his head back as he howled and pumped Eddie's mouth full of his sperm! Wolf grunted and growled deeply in his throat as the cum kept shooting from his cockhead. The muscles in his sweat drenched torso and abs flexed and rippled at his orgasm.

Finally, he sagged forward and pulled his cock from Eddie's mouth. Eddie just moaned for a second, and then looked up at his master. "Thank you, Sir." was all he said.

Danny looked down at him and told him; "We're not quite done yet, boy. You need another reminder, one that you will remember for a while, boy!"

Eddie could only say; "Yes Sir. Whatever you want, Master."

Danny removed the restraints from his slave's arms and ankles and then told him to stand. When Eddie was in front of his master, Danny told him; "Over here, boy" and led him to the stocks along the wall. Within minutes Eddie was secured in the stocks, bent over at the waist, his head and hands securely restrained, and his ankles spread and strapped to a metal spreader bar.

Danny went into his toy box and brought out a pair of hair clippers. Eddie moaned when he figured what his master was going to do to him. Eddie had a full head of thick, black hair. Danny plugged in the clippers and, turning them on, began to shear his helpless slave's head. He ran the clippers front to rear on Eddie's head, peeling his hair down to a short black stubble. Danny kept working until all the hair that was left was a two inch wide Mohawk stripe running front to rear down the middle of Eddie's head.

Danny released his slave from his bondage and told him to kneel. Eddie immediately dropped to his knees in the middle of the room. Danny stepped in front of him and said; "Look at me, boy!"

Eddie raised his head and looked directly into his master's eyes as Danny softly told him; "I was very disappointed and angry with you, boy. You hurt me very badly tonight. I thought you were trained better than that! I don't believe you did that! What in the fuck were you thinking, boy? Do you know how long it will take for my reputation to recover, boy?"

The tears were running down Eddie's face as he softly said in a quavering voice; "You don't know how very sorry I am, Master. I don't know what came over me, Sir. I truly wouldn't ever want to hurt you, Sir! I don't know what to say, Sir, except that I'm sorry! I know that it will take time before you could ever forgive me, but I'll do whatever it takes, Sir! I just want the chance to earn your forgiveness, Master!"

Danny stared down at the wretched boy cowering and groveling on the concrete floor of my torture chamber and in a voice that seemed to come from somewhere in the very depths of his soul, intoned; "Boy, you have lost all of your privileges for as long as I see fit. That means no phone calls, no television viewing, no going out to the bars, and no speaking unless spoken to first. You cannot use any of the furniture at home. You get to sleep on the floor until I say otherwise. Consider yourself as a new trainee slave undergoing your first months of training all over again, since it seems that it didn't take the first time! You are now less than a slave. You will have to work hard just to make it back up to the status of a slave. It'll be your problem to explain your haircut to your boss at the limo company."

Eddie just knelt on the floor weeping. He looked so abjectly miserable that it was hard not to feel some compassion for him, but I knew that Danny was correct in his treatment of his boy. The relationship between a master and his slave has to be based on mutual trust. The boy is trusting his master with total control of his body, knowing that if the master is irresponsible, he could severely injure his slave, or even cause death! On the other hand, the master is trusting his slave to show him the proper respect that is his due.

The relationship is rather like a marriage, both partners must respect the other. Eddie had broken one of the basic rules of that relationship, and now was paying the price. I knew from looking at Danny how much it was hurting him inside to have to treat his boy so harshly. I also knew that Danny really loved Eddie, as much as I loved Wolf, but he had to re-establish the boundaries of acceptable behavior for his boy.

Danny turned to me and asked; "Master Eric, do you think it's been punished enough tonight?" Eddie moaned softly when he heard himself being referred to as "it". That meant that his master didn't even consider his slave to be a "him" anymore.

I nodded and told Danny; "I think it's ready to consider how to start to make it up to you, Master Daniel. Maybe we should just leave it alone for the night to think about it. Do you want to stay here tonight, or are you gonna take it home with you?"

Danny thought for a moment and said; "I wouldn't mind staying here if that's all right with you, Master Eric, but I think we need to find someplace to store this thing so it can't get into any more trouble tonight."

I grinned at Eddie like a lion would grin at a cornered sheep and said; "Don't worry, I have just the place. Wolf, get the irons!"

Wolf walked over to a corner of the dungeon and retrieved a set of heavy slave shackles that were hanging on the wall. He held them for me as I unlocked the heavy steel collar and restraints attached to a length of thick chain.

I looked down at Eddie, still kneeling on the floor and told him harshly; "Up, you!"

He slowly rose to his feet and stood in front of me, head bent down, and his eyes on the floor. Danny stepped in and removed Eddie's studded leather slave collar and growled; "You'll get this back only when you've earned the right to wear it again."

I slipped the thick metal collar around Eddie's throat and closed it, locking it securely. Next his wrists were secured in equally thick metal wrist restraints fastened to the chain running down the front of his body from the collar. The restraints were fastened to the central chain with short lengths of chain that would not allow Eddie to touch his cock, or any other part of his own body except for a small portion of his chest. Finally, I ordered him to bend over at the waist to allow me to fasten ankle restraints on both of his legs.

The chain between the collar and his ankles was not long enough for Eddie to be able to stand upright, and the ankle restraints were so close together that he could only walk in a shuffling gait.

I led the hobbled, chained slave over to the cell built under the stairs coming down into the dungeon from the house. Two of the walls, and the floor of the cell were rough concrete, while the top of the cell was unfinished wood sloping down under the stairs to the floor. The fourth wall was iron bars welded together, with a narrow door for entry into the cell. I led the helpless slave into the cell and fastened a length of chain from an eyebolt in the wall to a ring welded to the back of the collar around his neck. I knew from more personal experience with Mike that the collar was very uncomfortable, with hard metal edges that dug into the neck and shoulders of whoever was wearing it.

The only furniture in the cell was a wooden bench about four feet long and about ten inches wide. Eddie was only going to be able to lie on his side on the bench in a fetal position, unable to stretch out full length due to the shortness of the chain.

Spending the night in the cell, shackled in the chains was very uncomfortable, to say the least! I knew, having spent many nights there myself.

I closed the cell door with a resounding clang that echoed through the dungeon. Eddie whimpered softly at the sound of the door being locked tightly. Danny looked down dispassionately at the miserable boy and snarled, "Shut the fuck up, punk! You earned this, so don't bitch about it, or you might find yourself spending two or three days here. Or if you would rather, we can take you someplace downtown and dump you out naked on a city street. Let's see you explain that to the cops, punk!"

At that, he turned on his heel and walked out, being followed by Wolf and myself. The last thing I did before heading up the stairs was to flip off the light, leaving the battered, broken and thoroughly miserable slave shackled in heavy chains and painful irons, locked in a small uncomfortable cell in total blackness. The final sound I heard as the door to the dungeon closed, was the heart-rending sound of Eddie finally breaking down completely, and beginning to cry once again, all alone in the dark.

Chapter Fifteen
The Challenge

The next morning, I awoke early even though Danny and I had stayed up late talking about Eddie's discipline and punishment. I had told Wolf to sleep in his own bed so Danny and I could have some time alone. I walked down into the dungeon to find Eddie curled up on the bench in the cell, sleeping fitfully. He looked thoroughly miserable, even in his sleep, so I figured that his punishment had taken.

When Danny and Wolf were awake, we had breakfast, cooked by Wolf as usual, and then took some eggs and ham down into the dungeon for Eddie. I had dumped the food into a stainless steel dog dish and I told the battered, exhausted slave that if he wanted to eat anything, he was going to have to figure out how to do it himself. Eddie just groaned as he knelt on the floor of the cell and buried his face in the bowl, licking up the food as best as he could. When he was done I unlocked the shackles and irons from his wrists and ankles, then unlocked his collar. Danny led him outside to the pool area.

Danny told Eddie; "You stink really bad, and you have food all over yourself. Get over by the wall and stand there!"

Eddie did as he was told, and stood, enduring having his master use the garden hose and spray him off with cold water. When Danny was done, Eddie knelt in front of him, shivering and whimpering with the cold. Danny looked down and said; "Well, are you ready to go home, so we can start your training all over again?" Eddie just nodded silently, and bent over to kiss his master's feet.

Danny led Eddie back upstairs where the both of them got dressed. As they were leaving, Danny told me, "Thanks for the use of your dungeon, Master Eric. I hope that being shackled up all night was enough to get this boy to start to remember his training!"

Eddie just stared at the floor, shamefaced and embarrassed.

I told Danny, "Any time you need to bring it back and work it over some more, just let me know. I have lots more things that we could do to it that would hurt a lot more than what we've already done!"

Danny just grinned and said, "Thanks, Eric. I'll remember that."

He then turned to his miserable boy and told him harshly, "You need to show Master Eric how you feel about him letting you stay in his dungeon all night, instead of throwing you out on the street, which was about all you deserved, punk!"

Eddie knelt in front of me, licking my boots, softly murmuring, "Thank you, Sir, for allowing me to stay the night, Sir."

I lifted his head up so he was looking into my eyes and snarled, "I just want you to know, punk, that if I ever see or hear of you disrespecting your master like that again, what you suffered last night will seem like a walk in the park! Is that understood, punk?"

Eddie's face crumpled, as he seemed on the brink of tears again as he silently nodded.

After they were gone, Wolf seemed to be a bit uncomfortable around me for the first time since we had been together. I finally asked him what was bothering him.

He replied; "Sir, that's the first time I can ever remember you being that upset with anyone. It just surprised me a bit. I'm not used to seeing you that way."

I sat down on the couch and told him to sit with me. I explained; "It wasn't that I was upset with Eddie personally, it was more that I was upset that he had disrespected his master so. I know that he was excited by the stories we were telling about the ranch, but he should have been able to remember his discipline and training, and not misbehave in public." I grinned at Wolf and said; "Of course, you'd never behave like that, now would you, boy?"

My smile faded as he looked at me and said in all seriousness; "I would hope not, Sir. And, if I ever did, I would expect you to punish me even harder than Eddie was punished!"

I looked into his deep, brown eyes, and told him; "Trust me, boy. If you ever did misbehave like that, you would learn what it means to suffer torture worse than anything you have ever had to endure. Just let that be a warning to you, boy."

Wolf nodded slowly as he considered what I had told him. Then I noticed the devilment creep back into his eyes as he jokingly said; "Let's see, what could I do that would be worse than that, so I could see just how much pain I could really take?"

I shot him one of my mock glares and snarled; "Just keep it up, smart-ass and it won't take much more for you to find out!"

He turned to me and said; "I've said it before, Sir, and I'll say it again. Promises, promises!" He gave me a look of such wide-eyed innocence that I couldn't help myself and burst out laughing. I pulled him to me and gave him a hug.

"Well boy, until you do screw up badly enough to be tortured like that, I've got something else to keep the both of us busy for a while. I've been thinking about trying to get back into competitive bodybuilding. Do you want to try training heavily enough to be able to compete along with me?"

Wolf's face split with a huge grin. "I'd love it, Sir! I'd love to be able to make everyone at the bars just go nuts with envy when I walk in at the end of a leash held by the hottest muscle master in the city."

I smiled at his enthusiasm, but I felt that I had to tell him the whole story about what we would be getting ourselves into.

"O.K. boy, but you know that there will be a great deal of hard work and strict training for the both of us, with a lot of effort. If we are gonna do this, I will need a total commitment from you, as I intend to commit myself to it totally, as well!"

Wolf nodded and said; "Yes Sir, I understand. I've done some training like that, but not since the last time I competed, way back when I was in High School."

I grinned at him. "Yeah, way back then. That must have been when dinosaurs ruled the Earth. Jeez, I've got socks that are older than you!"

We both laughed loud and long at that, the last vestiges of my bad mood dispelled by Wolf's gentle silliness. He always had the ability to cheer me up, no matter how cranky of a mood I was in. I pulled him to me and gave him a long hug.

"Well, we need to concentrate on what we will need to change in our training to be able to compete. I know that we're both in great shape, but competing at the level that we want to here is going to require a whole new workout plan, and a total commitment to winning our weight classes in whatever contest we get into. As a matter of fact, boy, here is the challenge you will face if you want to do this. If we both enter a contest, you have to do as well in your weight class as I do in mine, or you will face a night, or possibly an entire weekend of torture unlike anything you have ever faced. You are eight years younger than I am and you should be able to do better in a contest than I can. If I beat you, that only means that you have been goofing off, and I'll have no choice but to torture the laziness right out of you! Agreed, boy?"

Wolf thought for just a moment before saying; "Yes, Sir, I agree to your terms, Sir, but, what's in it for me if I beat you, Sir?"

I thought for a minute, gave him another hug, looked into his brown eyes and, giving him a smile, said; "If you beat me in whatever competition we enter, I'll be your slave for a whole month. How's that?"

Wolf chuckled, grinned and said, "I hope you're ready for some severe torture, slave, because I intend to beat the pants off of you in whatever contest we enter!"

I cuffed him playfully on the side of the head and grinned, "In the immortal words of Chuck, 'In your dreams, pansy boy!'"

Over the next few days we worked with some of the personal trainers at the gym we went to in town, and I checked out some of the latest nutritional and training info on the internet, until I had set up a strict training regimen for the both of us. The first few workouts we did with our new routines showed both of us where we had to work on our weak spots. My weakest features were my shoulders and lower back, while Wolf was lacking a bit in his legs. We were both better built than a large majority of the other guys in the city, but we were still a bit short of being in competition shape.

After a week or so of really killer workouts, I finally decided that it was time to take Wolf back down to the dungeon and start to work on his nipples again as a reward for his throwing himself into our new workouts so totally. The brandings had healed, leaving thick, reddish rings of scar tissue around his tits. The marks highlighted his nipples, making them stand out like the center rings of a bull's-eye. Wolf seemed to have a natural ability to heal quickly from any bumps, bruises, or any other marks I inflicted on his body.

That afternoon, after we had finished a heavy chest workout at the gym, I told Wolf not to bother showering at the gym, but just to collect our gym bags and put them in the car. I drove us home and led Wolf downstairs into the dungeon. Within minutes, he was stripped naked and strapped securely to the bondage table with thick leather straps around his wrists, biceps, waist, thighs and ankles. There was also a strap across his throat on top of his collar. He lay on the table, his pumped chest rising and falling with each breath, and his cock stiff and fully erect in anticipation of his first session of torture since our trip to the ranch, almost a month ago.

I stepped up in front of his helpless body, strapped to the table, and just gave him an evil smile.

"Well, boy, I think it's high time for you to remember what it's like to suffer! You've been just lazing around for almost a month now, but your break is at an end!"

Wolf just moaned softly; "Yes, Sir. Thank you, Sir!"

I reached out and began to roll Wolf's nipples between my fingers. He closed his eyes and gently moaned with pleasure at the feel of my hands working on his tits. I slowly increased the pressure and the stretching of his nipples, until he was groaning with that special combination of pain and pleasure that he loved so much.

After about ten minutes of manhandling his tits, I rotated the table until Wolf was almost standing upright. I went over to the shelves that held my toys and picked up the vacuum pump and the tubing and clear Lucite cylinders I used to enlarge Wolf's nipples. Wolf lay back on the table, his chest rising and falling rapidly as his body responded to the first torture he had to endure in quite a while. He moaned again softly as I set up the equipment on the small table next to the larger bondage board. The plastic hoses were attached to the pump and to the clear cylinders. Next, I ran a small bead of thick lube around the bottoms of the cylinders to ensure a good, airtight seal against Wolf's chest.

I turned on the pump and held one of the cylinders against his chest over Wolf's right nipple. Immediately the cylinder sealed itself against Wolf's solid pec, sucking his nipple up into the cylinder, and causing his tit to immediately begin to swell and enlarge. Wolf hissed between clenched teeth at the feel of his tit beginning to pump up. I repeated the process on his left tit, leaving Wolf lying helpless on the bondage board with his nipples rapidly enlarging and beginning to darken, as the blood was pulled into the flesh of his huge tits.

I stepped up to the bondage board and sneered down at Wolf; "You like that, boy?"

He moaned; "Oh God, yes, Sir! I've missed it so much, Sir!"

I gave him another wicked smile and told him; "Alright, boy, you like it so much, let's just see how much you like it in an hour!"

Wolf whimpered at that but I wasn't sure if he thought I was serious or not. I wasn't going to leave the pump working on his tits for much more than half an hour. I rarely left the pump on his tits for more than thirty minutes at a time, as his tits became incredibly sensitive from the constant sucking of the cylinders. Also, there was a small but real possibility of damage to his nipples from having the circulation cut off for an extended period of time. But, I figured that since Wolf hadn't had his tits pumped for a while, the chance of his being injured was small enough to be ignored. I knew that Wolf would signal me if he was in any real distress, or if he felt his tits going numb or felt any other signs of damage. Also, I just liked to mess with his head!

I turned without another word and strode to the door leading to the stairs up to the house. Just before I went thru, I turned back to Wolf strapped helplessly to the table and said; "See you later, slave!" I turned off the dungeon lights, leaving him bound in total darkness with the pump cylinders sucking relentlessly on his already swollen nipples.

I went upstairs to my room and stripped off my gym shorts and athletic shoes, and changed into just my chest harness and boots.

Naked other than the harness and boots, I waited a while before I went back down into the dungeon, where I turned the lights back on, revealing my slave strapped to the bondage table, his body gleaming with sweat and his nipples swollen and bloated by the vacuum cylinders.

Wolf moaned slightly as I walked past him without acknowledging him, and began to set up the equipment needed to continue his nipple torture. I brought over the small table and set it about five feet in front of the bondage table, directly under the beam in the ceiling with the eyebolts used for restraints. I next brought over two five gallon plastic buckets and set one on the floor in front of the table. The other one I took into the bathroom and filled with water and then lifted it up on top of the table. I ran a rope through a pulley hanging from one of the eyebolts in the beam between Wolf and the buckets.

Finally, it was time to start working on Wolf. I stepped up to him holding two long lengths of leather thronging. I turned the valve of the vacuum line on his left nipple off and slowly pulled off the cylinder, leaving his nipple hugely swollen and engorged. I wiped the lube off with a rag and then wrapped the thong around the base of his tit, tying it tightly and leaving about a foot of the leather hanging down his chest. Wolf groaned as I repeated the procedure on his other nipple, leaving his thick tits tightly tied off and swollen.

Next I took a six inch spreader bar and tied the thongs to the loops on the ends of the bar. The rope threaded through the pulley was tied to the loop in the middle of the bar. I pulled the rope tight, causing Wolf to moan and growl as his nipples were stretched slightly away from his pecs. He moaned again when I looped the rope thru the handle of the empty bucket and tied it off, leaving the bucket suspended about eight inches off of the floor. Wolf was moaning continuously now, but it was a moan of pleasure. His rock hard cock confirmed that he was in ecstasy, not agony. At least, not yet!

Wolf began to moan in earnest when he figured out what I was going to do to him when I took a small plastic tube and looped it from the upper bucket and hung it down into the lower one. Next I sucked on the tube to start a siphon of water from one bucket into the other.

I turned to my helpless slave and sneered at him; “Let’s see how you like it when the weight starts to really pull on those tits, boy. Think you can take forty pounds yanking on your tits, boy? I figure it’ll take about half an hour to move the water from one bucket into the other. I’m gonna love watching you suffer, slave!"

Wolf only moaned as he felt the weight begin to pull on his nipples harder and harder.

I pulled over my chair, sat down in front of Wolf and just watched his magnificent body strain against the restraints holding him to the table, as his nipples were slowly but inexorably stretched!

The moans and growls emanating from his throat slowly grew in volume and intensity as Wolf's tits were pulled further and further away from his chest as the weight in the bucket slowly got heavier and heavier.

Within fifteen minutes the moans turned into howls of agony as his nipples were tortured harder and harder with the constant pulling. They were stretched a good three or four inches from his gleaming pecs. His abs flexed erratically as he tried to breathe without moving his chest any more than he had to. His eyes were closed and his face bore its familiar look of pain mixed with intense concentration, as Wolf tried to endure the intense pain ripping through his body from his brutally tortured nipples!

The sweat was literally running down Wolf's bronze torso in constant streams from his pecs and heaving, washboard abs. His thick, straining arms also glistened in the heat of the torture chamber, as I pushed my willing slave to the outer edges of his ability to endure extreme nipple torture.

In just about another five minutes, Wolf was screaming constantly as his tits were stretched further than they had ever been pulled before. Just when I suspected that he couldn't take another pound of weight pulling on his tits, the stream of water sputtered to a stop. Wolf was supporting almost a full forty pounds by his nipples alone. I guess the water was running just a bit faster that I thought that it would.

I stepped up to my tortured slave and gently stroked a fingertip over both of his hugely swollen, stretched tits. Wolf howled even louder at even that slight touch on his incredibly sensitive nipples.

"Oh, so that hurts, does it, boy?" I sneered at my slave.

Wolf opened his eyes and weakly moaned; "Oh God, yes, Sir. It hurts so bad, Sir! I love it, Sir! Hurt me more, if you want, Sir, please! Torture me as hard as you want to, Sir! I've been bad, just lying around waiting to heal, Sir! I deserve whatever torture you want to force me to endure, Sir!":

Wolf knew that this type of begging would just turn me on so much that I would torture him right to the edge and then push him over from pleasure into the realm of total agony.

I stepped over to my toys on the shelves on the wall and picked up a pair of simple clothespins that the clamp ends had been coated in liquid latex. I opened one of the clothespins and set it on Wolf's right nipple. He shrieked in agony as the clothespin slowly clamped shut on his tit. I allowed him to accept the pain for just a few seconds before I repeated the procedure on his left nipple. He screamed constantly, his eyes squeezed tightly shut again and his head rolling back and forth as much as it could with the restraint across his throat.

I was incredibly turned on watching my slave shrieking and screaming in total agony, his magnificent physique straining and struggling futilely against the restraints holding him helpless as he was tortured. His abs were flexing and rippling as he was forced to try to breathe without moving his chest, as even the slightest movement caused fresh waves of pain to rip throughout his body from his nipples.

Wolf's cock was absolutely rock hard as he was being tortured. The pre-cum was running down the throbbing shaft from his piss-hole, showing me that even though Wolf was screaming in total agony, he was also turned on by the pain he was being forced to endure with no hope of escape.

Right then I decided to take my boy right to the edge and then beyond.

I snarled to him; "Open your eyes, slave! You need to see what's coming up next. I want you to anticipate just how much you're gonna hurt in just a few minutes, slave!"

Wolf moaned as he opened his now bloodshot eyes and watched helplessly as I walked over to the suspended bucket and started to drop my six ounce lead weights in. He shrieked at the top of his lungs as each weight added to the already excruciating pull on his tits. After five weights were added, he screamed; "Yellow, Sir. Please!"

"Yellow" was one of our code words. It meant that he didn't want me to release him, but he couldn't take any more intensity of whatever torture he was being subjected to at the time. I immediately stopped adding weights but didn't make any move to release him, or ease his torment in any way. I knew that Wolf was almost deliriously happy with pain, and was in the grip of an incredible endorphin high!

Wolf was gasping for air as he was almost unable to breathe with the brutal pulling on his nipples and pecs. The sight of his terrific body enduring such an impossible level of agony was such a turn-on to me that I couldn't resist any more. I knelt under the rope stretching Wolf's tits and sucked his throbbing, streaming cock into my mouth. Wolf moaned even louder when I started to stroke my hands lightly over his washboard abs, which felt like a silk covered brick wall.

Finally, he shrieked in total pain when I flicked my fingers over the clothespins on the tips of his brutalized nipples, snapping them again and again! His abs flexed in front of my eyes while I tortured his nipples beyond anything I had ever done to them before.

Wolf slammed his head back against the padded bondage table with an audible "Thud" as he finally came, filling my mouth with a huge, hot load of his sperm. He shrieked again and again as I unclipped the clothespins from his tortured nipples, his muscled body straining at the limits of his strength!

His scream of "AAAUUGGGHHH!! OOOHH FFFUUCCCKKK!!!" filled the torture chamber as I brutally squeezed and twisted Wolf's battered, swollen tits. The sperm seemed to keep shooting out of his cock into my mouth for as long as I continued to torture his nipples, but I knew it was really only for a matter of moments. The intensity of Wolf's orgasm made it seem to last much longer.

Finally, I released my agonized slave's bruised, mauled nipples, drawing a relieved gasp from him. I stood up and slowly lifted the weighed, water-filled bucket with one hand while I untied the rope from the handle with the other hand.

Wolf moaned again as the pull finally eased from his tits, but then he began to scream in agony again as I untied the leather thongs from his pecs, and the blood rushed back into his brutalized nipples. I leaned in and began to gently lick his tits, each touch of my tongue tearing another agonized scream from Wolf's throat. He shrieked again and again while I was licking and sucking on the two points of agony on his chest that seemed to be consuming his whole being!

The licking torture continued for just a few more minutes, before I stood up, and rotated the table so that Wolf was now head down at about a forty-five degree angle to the floor.

"Open your mouth, slave!" I snarled at him. Wolf's mouth flew open and I drove my throbbing cock deeply into his throat. I was so turned on by watching Wolf endure the brutal torture of his nipples that I shot a huge load within a minute of starting to rape his mouth.

I growled and snarled deeply in my throat as my load filled my slave's hot mouth, his tongue flicking across my cockhead. When I finally pulled back from him, Wolf just gasped a soft; "Thank you, Sir."

I immediately rotated the table back into its almost upright position and stepped up to my helpless, bound slave.

"Did I say that you could speak, boy?" I snarled into his ear, even as I grabbed both of his nipples again and twisted the incredibly tender knots of flesh as hard as I could!

The cords and veins popped out on Wolf's throat as he screamed as loud as he could at the burst of pain in his chest.

"AAAAUUUGGGGHHH!! OOOHH FFFUUUCCCCKKKK! SIRRR! I'M SORRY SIR!!" he shrieked!

I let go of his nipples, and Wolf immediately slumped forward, only held on the table by the restraints across his body. Immediately, I rotated the table back horizontal, and began to un-strap my now only semi-coherent slave. I listened to the rasp of his breath in his throat, and decided that he was breathing all right, but that I had just pushed him over the edge of his capacity to endure pain. Within moments, Wolf began to weakly moan as his now reddened eyes fluttered open.

I smiled down at him and said; "Well boy, do you remember your discipline now? I bet you won't do that again, will you?"

He swallowed a couple of times before he could hoarsely gasp out; "No Sir, I'm sorry, Sir."

I bent down over him and kissed him on the mouth. "Did you enjoy yourself, boy?"

He grinned weakly. "Oh God, yes, Sir! That was great, Sir! Thank you, Sir!"

I smiled back down at him again as I finished un-strapping him from the table. I helped Wolf sit up on the edge of the table, and then supported him as he stood up.

I grinned at him and told him; "Well boy, that was just a sample of what you will have to endure if you don't do better than I do in any contests we enter. I hope that it was enough encouragement to really get serious about working out. If you don't beat me, or at least tie me, you'll endure the same torture, except you will have a bucket attached to each nipple. Just imagine twice as much weight pulling on each tit!"

Wolf shivered briefly at the thought, and then dropped to his knees in front of me.

He looked earnestly up into my eyes and said; "Master, I promise to do my best to win any contest we enter. If I don't, I deserve to be forced to endure whatever torture you want to subject me to!"

At that, he bent over and started to lick my boots. As he was cleaning my boots, I saw his back begin to shudder with the delayed reaction to the pain he had been forced to endure as Wolf began to cry, sobbing loudly as he worked on the shiny black leather with his tongue. I allowed him to clean my boots for as long as he felt it was necessary for him to do so, then I ordered him to his feet, and gathered my exhausted slave into my arms and held him tightly.

"Let's go upstairs and clean up, boy." I told him gently, "And then we can rest up and get ready to back to the gym tomorrow for more working out. Back and shoulders, boy!"

Wolf grinned up into my eyes and said; "Yes Sir. I just hope you're ready to get beaten in any contest we go into, because that's exactly what I'm gonna do!"

"Oho- a challenge, huh boy? That's twice now that you've said that! Just remember one of my cardinal rules- Old age and treachery can beat youth and skill any day!" I grinned into my lover's face as he totally broke up laughing at my taunt. Right then I knew that the gauntlet had been cast down, and that we were both in this competition for real, not just as master and slave, or even as lovers, but as two bodybuilders out to win. This was going to be fun. The extra pain and humiliation that the loser would have to endure was just icing on the cake!

Chapter Sixteen
Wolf's Tale

Wolf whimpered softly as I helped him up the stairs from the dungeon into the main part of our house. The pain was probably still shooting throughout his entire torso from his tortured nipples. I figured that they would be really tender for two or three days at the least. Now that the endorphin rush was beginning to subside, I knew that the pain in his chest would start to really kick in. The same thing used to happen to me whenever Mike would work me over really hard.

I helped Wolf into the bathroom, holding him against me in the shower for a while, as the warm water flowed over both of our bodies. After we had relaxed under the water for a while, I told Wolf just to take it easy for a bit while I fixed us a light dinner. I knew that it wouldn't be a good idea for him to eat too much for a while, as his body was still reacting to the pain of his torture.

When we had eaten, I suggested that we needed to go just rest for a bit on the couch. Wolf sighed as he snuggled up to me in our usual position for relaxing together, me sitting in the corner of our L-shaped couch, Wolf leaning back against my chest while sitting between my legs. I wrapped my arms around his hard body, holding him for a bit before I brought up the subject I wanted to talk about.

"I seem to remember that you said that you would tell me about your past, if I told you about mine. I've done my part, now it's time for you to do yours, boy." I told him with a grin. "O.K., time to fess up about your twisted youth!"

Wolf just gave me one of his fake, theatrical groans, saying in a whining voice; "Aw gee, Sir, do I really have to?"

I playfully cuffed him on the side of the head, sternly saying; "You bet, boy! Now, start talking!"

He turned, grinning at me, and began; "I was born on an Apache Indian reservation just outside of Phoenix, Arizona. My dad had owned a hardware store that was in one of the towns on the reservation, but really didn't follow too much of what went on with the tribal councils and so forth. He felt that the tribal government was trying to stay too much in the past, while he always was looking out for the future. As a result, I wasn't too popular with some of the other kids in the schools there. Their parents thought that I would be some sort of bad influence on them or something, I guess. I was involved with some of the cultural groups, such as the traditional dance groups and the like, and I became fluent in Apache and Spanish, as well as English, but I also spent a lot of time alone. Also, I knew from an early age that I was always more interested in other guys than in girls. That also set me apart from most of the other kids my age. The fact that my dad had married outside of the tribal group was also a problem for some of the older members of the community."

"Finally, it got so bad that my family moved from the reservation lands into a small town on the other side of Phoenix, so Dad would still be able to deal with the same suppliers for his business. It was there that I had some of the first experiences with sex with other guys that I ever had. Some of my cousins from my mom's side of the family came to visit when I was about 14 years old, taking me camping in the hills around the area. One day, three or four of the other guys were kind of messing around, teasing me about being the "savage Indian" as they put it. I was used to this kind of kidding, and I really didn't get offended by it. I was the only member of the family that had any Indian heritage and family, so I figured I would be treated a little differently."

"Somehow the discussion wandered around to the subject of Indians capturing white men and what they would do them. The oldest of my cousins, a guy named Miguel, suggested that I needed to be tied to a tree and tortured to see if "Indians can really take it as well as they can dish it out." as he put it. All the other guys were older and a lot bigger than me, so fighting them wasn't going to do any good."

"Within about five minutes, they had me stripped, tied to a tree on my knees, with my back against the trunk. Miguel reached into his pocket, pulled out a pair of clothespins, which he clipped to my tits. I tell you, my cock had never gotten so hard so fast."

"All the other guys started to joke about my hard on. Miguel said, "Well, I guess I know what he wants." The next thing I knew, he had taken his fat cock out of his pants, stuffing it into my mouth. He stood there fucking my mouth, until he shot a load of cum. That was the first time anyone had ever cum in my mouth, and I realized right then and there that I loved it!"

I grinned at Wolf as I said, "So that's what put you on the road to complete depravity, huh, boy? I guess I'll have to thank your cousin if I ever meet him for helping to create the sick and twisted individual that I love so much."

Wolf looked at me and sadly shook his head, saying seriously, "I don't think you would want to do that, Sir. We saw each other three or four more times on camping trips, but finally one time Miguel came over and asked me if I wanted to go with him to see some friends of his in town. I thought that it would be an opportunity to hang out with some older, cooler guys! What ended up happening was he and about five of the guys he hung out with took me over to an apartment that one of his friends had in Phoenix. They took me inside, force-stripped me, tied me over a table, and took turns raping me in both the ass and the mouth for about the next couple of hours!"

I was absolutely stunned at this news. "Oh, Shit!"

Wolf continued, "The worst part was that while one of the guys was fucking my ass and another was screwing my mouth, Miguel took off his belt and began beating me across the back with it. The pain was bad, but I was shocked when I realized I enjoyed it! I was only fifteen at the time, and all of them were at least eighteen or nineteen years old. I've never told anyone about that until now, Sir. When they were done, Miguel pulled out a gun, stuck the barrel in my mouth, and threatened to blow the back of my head off if anyone ever found out about it!"

Wolf's voice shook as he told me about his rape. All I could do was hold my lover and comfort him silently as he relived the ordeal.

After a few minutes I told him, "I'm sorry that ever happened to you. I never imagined that something so awful could have ever been done to you, boy. Is there anything I can do for you now?"

Wolf just shook his head, wrapped his arms around me, beginning to softly cry. I just held him until he cried himself out.

He lifted his head and looked at me with red-rimmed eyes, saying, "I'm sorry, Sir. I just never thought that bringing it up would bother me so much, but I'm all right now. I guess telling someone about it was something I've needed to do for a long time. You are the only person that I could ever tell, Sir. The last I ever heard of Miguel, he was in prison for robbing a liquor store and shooting the clerk. I just hope that he's getting some of the same treatment in jail that I got from him and his gang! He claims to be straight, but I really don't believe that. After all, he was the first mouth fuck I ever had!"

"Anyway after that, I went a while before I could have any more sex with other guys. I used to spend a lot of time alone hiking in the hills. I would sometimes fantasize about the types of tortures that might have been done to settlers and white men in the hills by the Indian tribes that used to live there. I occasionally would try tying myself up as best as I could and then would endure being in the sun and heat as long as I could before I would jack off."

"It wasn't until I got into high school that I started having sex on a regular basis with a few other guys there. Also, it was in high school that I discovered that my body would respond really well to weightlifting. I was on the wrestling team and started to work out to bulk up for wrestling. I wasn't really interested in trying to go out for football, and, to tell the truth, I thought that I might get to have a bit of fun with other guys wrestling. I mean, hot sweaty, almost naked men wrestling? What's not to like?"

I laughed at Wolf's expression. "Feeling better now, boy?" I asked him.

Wolf smiled and said, "Yes, Sir. Finally telling someone makes me feel better!"

I told him, "You know, I thought that you were somewhat twisted since the first day I ever saw you, boy. Now I think I know why."

Wolf just gave me a chuckle. I knew then that he would be all right. His usually happy nature would help him overcome the trauma of recalling his rape. I think he knew that I would help him any way I could.

I asked him, "Did that picture of you that I like so much come from when you were wrestling in school?"

He grinned, "Not exactly. It was taken by a friend of mine that I used to wrestle with, and I used to have sex with on a regular basis after I graduated from high school. We were both members of a gay wrestling club in the Phoenix area that I joined after I graduated and got my own place to live. He took the picture just before I pinned him in a match and gave him one of the best fuckings I've ever done to someone before I met you, Sir! I was about twenty when that picture was taken, so it was after high school."

I smiled at his enthusiasm. The picture was one of my favorites. It showed Wolf sitting in a wrestling ring wearing just a blue and black pair of Speedos and white athletic shoes, with his hair flowing down over his left shoulder from over a black bandanna tied around his head. The expression on his face shows that he was trying to look serious for the camera, but I could see the faintest hint of a smile on his face, and a look of devilish fun in his eyes. Since we had been together, Wolf had put on about fifteen pounds of pure muscle, was a lot bulkier, more ripped and defined than in the picture, but I still loved it since it showed his personality so perfectly.

Wolf continued, "I had a lot of fun with my friends in the wrestling group. It also turned out that some of the guys were members of the local leather club. I was still too young to join the club formally, but some of the members still used to tie me up and torture me pretty regularly. They were pretty good at bondage and torture, but none of them were as good as you, Sir! I got my first fucking since my rape from one of the leathermen, and I was impressed at how sensitive he was. I could only tell him that I had had a bad experience, and he was really gentle and considerate of my feelings. I guess that's when I really knew that I wanted to be a slave boy to a good leather master one day. Now, I'm the permanent slave to the best master in all of San Francisco, Sir!"

I couldn't say anything around the lump that had formed in my throat. I just wrapped my arms tighter around my boy and hugged him to my chest. We just sat there silently for a while, enjoying the closeness of each other.

Finally Wolf started his story again. "I was still living with my parents while I was in high school and trying to keep from them the fact that I was gay. They knew that the time I spent practicing with the wrestling team was school related, so I did have an excuse for being out a lot. I hated to have to mislead my parents, but they were both rather old fashioned on the subject of homosexuality, so I figured it would just be easier if they didn't know."

"What they noticed, as I did, was that the weightlifting I was doing as part of the workouts with the wrestlers, was really having an effect. I was getting really well built and buff, for only being about sixteen years old. I did enter a local high school bodybuilding contest in my senior year, winning first place in the novice category. That's the trophy in the case in the den, Sir, along with all your trophies."

I smiled at Wolf, "Well, we all have to start somewhere, boy. I didn't try a bodybuilding contest until I was with Mike, so I started later than you."

Wolf smiled back and said, "Yeah, and I'm betting that you were always bigger than me, Sir, so it was easier for you to win. Anyway, the only member of my family who knew that I was gay was my grandfather. He told me that he had known since the first time he ever saw me, when I was about six weeks old. I think I told you once that he was a shaman. He told me that he saw in my future not only the fact that I was gay, but that I would have a period of great troubles, then I would have great happiness later."

Wolf looked somber as he told me, "I thought for a while that the time of troubles was when I was raped, but I figured out later that it referred to the death of my parents."

I asked him, "Do you want to tell me what happened to them, or not? I won't be offended if you want to keep it to yourself."

Wolf shook his head and said, "No, I want to tell you, Sir. After all, you told me what happened to your family."

He sighed, sitting silently for a few minutes, as if to gather his thoughts before he could tell me the story of what happened to his parents.

"I had my own place on the outskirts of Phoenix, about ten miles from where my parents were living. It was just a small apartment, but it was the first place I had that was my own. One evening I had a friend from the leather club over. He had me tied to the bed spread-eagled, working on my tits and cock, when I thought I heard the sound of the door to my apartment opening through the hood on my head. I heard the guy working on me say 'What the hell?' and then I heard my mom shriek, "*Madre Con Dios*" and my dad just say 'Oh, Shit!'!"

"They had decided to pay me a visit, since they were in the area, but unfortunately they didn't call first. The guy who had me tied up released me as quickly as he could, but my folks had already left. I drove over to their house as fast as I could to try to explain what was going on. We had to just sit down together for a few hours and talk out my situation.

I could tell that they still didn't really understand or approve of my life, but they both told me that they still loved me, and that they would try to accept me as their gay son."

Wolf gave me a sad smile and continued, "I thought that we actually came to some kind of an unspoken understanding. I wouldn't bring up my private life, and they wouldn't question me about it. It wasn't the best situation we could have, but it was the best that we were going to get! We continued this way for the next eight or nine months, until the night that my folks were on their way back from a business trip up to Flagstaff. It was a cold night, and the car hit a patch of ice on the interstate. Dad apparently lost control of the car and it went over an embankment. I got a call from the state police telling me about the accident at about two in the morning. The only person I could call was my grandfather. He surprised me by telling me that he was expecting me to call him. He knew something had happened but didn't know exactly what!"

I held Wolf tightly as the tears began to flow down his face again. I knew the trauma of losing both parents tragically, and I was determined to support my boy any way I could.

After a few more minutes, Wolf seemed to calm down a bit. I got him some tissues and a glass of water, so he could compose himself. I just let him take his time, as I knew he would continue when he felt up to telling me more of his story. We just sat silently for a few more minutes, until Wolf rather unexpectedly said, "You know, Sir, The worst thing that affected me about the death of my parents wasn't the fact that they were killed in the car accident, even though that was really tragic, no, the worst thing that happened to me was what happened after they died! About two weeks after their funerals, I got a call from my dad's lawyer, telling me that he was going to do the reading of the will. I wasn't really too concerned about what was going to happen, since I was an only child. I don't want to sound mercenary or anything, but I figured that the will would leave most of my parent's things to me."

"You might imagine my surprise when the will actually left instructions that most of their assets were to be sold off, and the money to be given to various charities and the tribal council on the reservation where we used to live. All I got was a thousand dollars, and a letter from my folks telling me that they were shocked and disgusted by my lifestyle!"

I could actually feel Wolf's body shaking with repressed anger as he told me about his parent's betrayal of his trust. He had been honest with them after they found out he was gay, but they had secretly held it against him, cutting him almost totally out of their legacy. I could understand his anger and reluctance to tell me what they had done. I had seen my slave happy, sad, depressed, and on one memorable occasion, drunk, but I had never seen him almost totally consumed by a blind fury. This was a side of my lover that I hadn't seen and I didn't like it! Sadly, I didn't know what to do except to hold him tightly while waves of anger and rage flowed through him.

After almost ten minutes of bitter tears and shaking rage, I felt Wolf finally begin to calm down, having cried himself out for the second time within an hour. I held him tighter and softly murmured in his ear, "I'm so sorry, boy. What can I do to help?"

He snuffled a couple of times and looked at me through red-rimmed eyes. "Actually, Sir, I just think I need you to just be here with me a while."

"Don't worry, boy," I told him softly, "I'm not going anywhere. I'll be here for you as long as you want me to be."

We just sat silently for a while longer while I thought about what Wolf had revealed to me this evening. There was so much about my slave that I still didn't know. I decided then and there that I would continue to support him in any way that I could, both financially and emotionally.

In a few more minutes Wolf began to talk again, continuing his story.

"I was really upset with the whole somewhat homophobic mindset of anyone I talked to whenever I went back to the reservation to visit my grandfather, so I decided that I was just going to sell off most of whatever possessions that I had, and just travel. Some Indian tribes actually revered anyone who was gay, thinking it was a gift from the various gods, but most Apaches actually hated homosexual tribesmen, and banished them, or worse. I got rid of my car and all my furniture, just bought a backpack and hit the road, hitchhiking. I traveled around a lot of the southwest for a while, about a year or so, before I finally made it to San Francisco. I wasn't really happy with what had become of my life by then. I was almost broke, and had to resort to hustling for a while just to be able to eat."

Wolf looked shame-faced at the disapproving look that I shot him at that admission. He had never told me that he had hustled sex for money before.

"I only ever did it about three times, and I was always safe. I only let guys suck my cock until I came, and I never got fucked or ever fucked anyone else. I knew it was wrong, but when you're hungry enough, you'll do whatever you can. It was during this time that I went into the Eagle for the first time, and saw you with some of your friends and a boy in a collar. The very first time I saw you, I instantly knew you were the man I needed in my life! I mean, I saw your blue eyes, and your blonde hair, the way you commanded the boy you had, and everything else, and I just knew, Sir. Even so, I was afraid to try to talk to you since you were with someone else, so I just hid in the darker corners whenever you walked near me. The next time I saw you there, you had a different boy with you. I asked some of the bartenders about you. They told me that you didn't really have a full time slave boy. It was right then that I decided to talk to you the next time I ever saw you."

"As luck would have it, the very next time I was in the bar was that hot Sunday afternoon. It was also the first time I had seen you just wearing a vest without a shirt on under it, and I was absolutely amazed by your muscles, that was the final push that I needed to take my courage in my hands and come over and talk to you, Sir!"

Wolf grinned at me, kissed me and said, "I guess the rest is history, right Sir?"

I smiled back at him, saying; "History is always being written, boy. I think we have a lot more to write together!"

I leaned back on the couch holding Wolf tightly, his bare back pressed against my chest, just thinking about all the events in my lover's past that I had just learned. I knew that Wolf had a strong will to be able to endure the tortures I submitted him to, but I never realized how strong it was until now. I wasn't sure that I could have endured what he had endured growing up. We had both lost our parents under tragic circumstances, but Wolf had also had to endure a rape, a betrayal of faith by his parents, and the rejection of his lifestyle by almost his entire community!

After just sitting for a while, I leaned forward and told Wolf, "Let's go downstairs for a while. I think you really need to relax for a while boy. You're completely tensed up."

He just nodded and stood up. Taking him by the hand, I led my lover down into the side room of the dungeon that was near the sauna. I flipped on the power to the sauna and turned on the stereo, putting on some relaxing music, and unfolded my massage table that was leaning against the wall. I told Wolf to get on the table, face down. When he was in position, with his face down in the ring of padding on one end of the table, I flipped his hair forward and began to rub his thick shoulder muscles with my self-warming massage oil. Wolf almost purred with pleasure as my fingers dug deeply into the bunched muscles, knotted with tension.

After a few minutes of work, I felt the muscles in his shoulders and back begin to relax. I spent the next forty-five minutes giving my lover a deep massage from his ears all the way down to the soles of his feet. I loved the feel of his silky skin and his hard muscles under my hands as I worked on his body. When I was done, I softly whispered in Wolf's ear, "Whenever you can, turn over so I can do the other side."

Wolf just moaned softly and very slowly rolled himself over. I told him to make himself comfortable and began to repeat the entire massage up the front of his body, starting with his feet. I knew he was in total bliss by the soft whimpering moans of total pleasure that he made whenever I would begin to massage a different muscle group. Surprisingly, however, he was so totally relaxed that his cock stayed soft and limp.

It took almost an hour and a half to totally complete his massage, by the end of which I was totally soaked with sweat. When I was done, I told Wolf to sit up whenever he had the strength to do so. He lay on the table for about five minutes before slowly sitting up and swinging his legs over the side.

"Can you stand up, boy?" I asked him. He slowly stood up and then arched his back and stretched, every muscle rippling under his bronze skin.

"God, you're sexy!" I told him, kissing him deeply. Wolf returned the kiss, grinned his lopsided grin and said, "So are you, Sir. So are you!"

"Come on" I said, holding open the door to the sauna. We went in and sat down on two towels I had put on the bench when I turned on the heat. Within minutes we were both dripping with sweat in the 180 degree heat.

"Oh God, this feels great!" Wolf moaned, leaning back, putting his hands behind his head.

I reached out and gently stroked my fingertips down his chest and abs, saying; "Yeah, and it looks great, too!"

Wolf just moaned again when I leaned forward and gently began to suck on his still tender nipples, working my way back and forth across his chest. I worked the swollen nubs of flesh with my mouth and nipped them gently with my teeth until I felt Wolf's hand on the back of my head pressing my face tighter to his gleaming chest.

"Oh God, yes!" he hissed as I increased the pressure on his tits with my teeth.

I chewed his tits for a good five minutes while the sweat poured off of our bodies, until Wolf finally murmured, "Oh shit, Sir, I can't take any more! Please stop!"

I moved my mouth from Wolf's nipples, slowly working my way down his torso until I could suck his thick cock into my mouth. Wolf gasped "Oh God" and began to thrust his dick between my lips until he pumped a load of his thick cum into my mouth.

Swallowing my lover's load, I sat up and kissed him deeply. Wolf finally said; "Sir could we get out of here? It's really hot, and I'm feeling a bit light-headed."

"Sure, boy, let's go." We went out into the dungeon and headed for the small bathroom to get a quick shower. When we were both rinsed off, I led Wolf outside onto the deck around the pool and over to the hot tub. The water wasn't too hot since the heater hadn't been on for too long, but the swirling action of the water felt absolutely wonderful and the gentle warmth of the water contrasted with the chill of the late September air.

We sat in the tub for a while, my arms wrapped around Wolf's hard, young body, while we watched the fog roll in over the bay. I just thought about all the things that Wolf had revealed to me tonight, then I made a decision that I had been contemplating for several weeks, ever since our experiences at the ranch.

"Carlos, I want to tell you something." I said to him. He turned and faced me, neck deep in the water, his hair floating around his shoulders. I think he knew something was up, as I almost never called him anything but Wolf.

"I can understand how you would feel betrayed by others, seeing what happened to you in the past, but I want to let you know that nothing like that will ever happen to you again, as long as I am alive. Tomorrow, you and I will go into town and talk to my lawyer. I've been thinking about writing up a new will, and since there is no one else in my life I care about as much as you, and I have no other family, you will be taken care of for the rest of your life. You have allowed me to mark you as my property, and I want to do something for you in return. Neither one of us really has any other close family, so from now on, we are each other's family, if that's all right with you."

Wolf just looked at me for a moment, finally moving in, wrapping his arms around me, and hugging me tightly. With tears beginning to stream down his face, he said in a quavering voice; "Oh God. Thank you, Sir! I never expected anything like that, Sir."

He then kissed me as deeply and as passionately as he had ever done in all the time we had been together. I held on to him as he began to cry, this time with happiness, his entire body shaking and quivering with emotion. I let my lover cry himself out again, just holding and comforting him as he finally let go of all the emotions and feelings he had kept buried deeply inside himself for all those years.

When Wolf finally calmed down, he turned his face to me and said; "Sir, I want you to know that I'll never knowingly do anything to disappoint you, or to make you regret having chosen me to be your slave!"

I smiled down at him and told him; "I don't think you ever could disappoint me, boy. Not unless you really worked at, that is! Now, let's go to bed, boy. It's been a long day, and I'm getting tired."

Wolf smiled and said; "Me too."

We clambered out of the hot tub, rinsing off before heading upstairs. Later, after Wolf had sucked a load of cum from my cock before drifting off to sleep, I reflected on our time together and the changes both of us had gone through. I had someone to care for, someone who needed me for an anchor in his life, and I felt that Wolf now had a substitute family in me and my friends in the leather community to help him grow and mature into the strong individual I knew he would become.

As I dropped off into sleep, my last thoughts were about the future that Wolf and I were going to share together, with all of its unknowns, and its promises. I hoped that it would be a good future. With Wolf there at my side, I just knew that it would be!

Epilogue
Several Months Later...

I stood in the dungeon feeling the solid wood of the St. Andrews cross pressing against my back and legs, a feeling I hadn't felt for a while, but had never totally forgotten.

My sensations were limited to only what I could feel, as my head was covered by my tight leather hood, eliminating my sight, blocking my hearing, and preventing me from speaking.

The impossible had happened; Wolf had beaten me in the bodybuilding contest! It was almost unheard of for a middleweight bodybuilder to beat a heavyweight in the final pose-off, but that's what happened. He had only beaten me by a very few points in the final judging, but he beat me nonetheless. Now I had to make good on my bet with him by serving as his slave for a month!

I remembered what he had told me after the results were announced. We hugged on stage as the winner and first runner up. Then I realized that I had lost to him. Wolf had just grinned his crooked smile, saying "I hope you're ready for some pain!"

All I could do once we were home, was to strip at his order, kneel in front of him and wait silently while Wolf buckled a slave collar around my throat. He led me down into the torture chamber, spread-eagling me on the cross. After I was secured to the cross, Wolf placed the hood over my head. Just before inserting the gag in the mouth hole of the hood and lacing the hood tight, he asked me, "What to you want, slave?"

I could only answer one way, "Master Carlos, I want you to torture me! I lost and I deserve to be punished! Please, Sir, torture me!"

He pushed the leather gag into my mouth and fastened it to the hood. The hood tightened around my head as the laces were pulled tight. I felt his strong fingers stroke down my chest and begin to twist my nipples...

TO BE CONTINUED!

About the Author

Alan Weyant grew up on the west coast of Florida. After graduating from high school, he served stints in both the U.S. Merchant Marine, and the U.S. Navy.

He lived in the Tampa Bay area before relocating to his current home, on 5 rural acres of wooded riverfront property in southern Kentucky, next door to his lover's 14 acres. Alan has been active in both the leather community, as a lifetime associate member of The Adventurers leather club of Florida, and in the bear community, as a former member of The Growlers of Tampa Bay.

He is an over-the-road long distance truck driver. His interests include weightlifting, reading science fiction, plus he is an avid bicyclist, carrying his bike with him in his truck, allowing him to ride wherever he finds himself in the country.

www.ingramcontent.com/pod-product-compliance
Lightning Source LLC
Chambersburg PA
CBHW071219260626
47162CB00004B/1363

* 9 7 8 1 9 3 4 6 2 5 1 0 1 *